IN THE VOID

Borgo Press Books by MICHAEL R. COLLINGS

IN THE VOID

POEMS OF SCIENCE FICTION, MYTH AND FANTASY, & HORROR

by

Michael R. Collings

Emeritus Professor of English
Seaver College, Pepperdine University

Foreword by Orson Scott Card

Translation by Robyn Stewart with Alan Anderson

THE BORGO PRESS

An Imprint of Wildside Press LLC

MMIX

Borgo Laureate Series
ISSN 1082-3336

Number Five

www.wildsidebooks.com

FIRST EDITION

CONTENTS

MYTH AND FANTASY

HORROR

APPENDIX

ACKNOWLEDGMENTS

Many thanks to Orson Scott Card for his kind permission to print "The Poetic Audience" as the introduction to this book.

And many thanks to Robyn Stewart for permission to print the Klingon translation of "The Last Pastoral."

Some poems in this collection have been published, often in different form, in the following collections by Michael R. Collings: *Naked to the Sun* (1985, 2007), *Dark Transformations* (1990, 2007), *Nestlings of a Dark God* (1996,1999), and *The Art and Craft of Poetry* (2009); and in the following: *Aliens and* Lovers, edited by Millea Kenin; *Being*; *California Quarterly*; *Dreams and Nightmares*; *Gaslight*; *Midnight Zoo*; *Next Phase*; *Owlflight*; *Poet*; *Redrum Coffeehouse* (online); *Rouge et Noir #6*; *Scifaiku* (Online); *Space & Time*; *Star*Line* (Science Fiction Poetry Association); *Studia Mystica*; *The Barrelhouse*; *The Blood Review*; *The Lamp-Post of the Southern California C. S. Lewis Society; The Leading Edge* (Brigham Young University); *The Magazine of Speculative Poetry*; *O-Negative*; *Undinal Songs*; *Ygdrasil* (online).

FOREWORD

THE POETIC AUDIENCE

by Orson Scott Card

I have a question to ask.

Why isn't Michael Collings a rock star?

I ask this in all seriousness. I have been reading and enjoying his poetry for years. If these were songs, he would have album after album, each with a few hit singles for the masses, surrounded by many cuts whose subtleties were appreciated by connoisseurs.

I have heard him read his own poems and the poems of others; but these readings should have been in crowded arenas, with the audience raising their hands to shine tiny torches in silent reverence while he read old favorites, then cheering thunderously, stamping their feet, at the end of the premiere performance of a poem he had read for the first time ever, just for them.

Instead, the publication of any book of poetry these days is a matter of little public notice. Only within the tiny community of university poets are a few stars recognized. Yet even these "stars" make barely a bump in the vast plain of public fame.

* * * * * * *

When I think of readers in the early 1800s swooning over the poetry of Byron, Keats, and Shelley as if they were Elvis or the Beatles, I can't help but wonder what happened to that passionate audience.

Is it simply a matter of technology? In the age before records and radio (or CDs and the Internet), was poetry merely a place-holder, ready to be supplanted as soon as a means of distributing three-minute songs was invented?

Could it be a decline in the quality of education? Because children are no longer taught to memorize, no longer given real poetry to read, taught to write haikus instead of metrical verse, have we deliberately raised two generations of poetic cripples?

Or did the audience not really disappear at all? Perhaps there is never more than a tiny portion of the populace that will care for poetry, but in those halcyon days of general illiteracy, they made up a much higher proportion of those who could read and write.

Or—and this is the possibility that terrifies modern poets—is it possible that poetry has decayed to the point where it's not *worth* the attention of a large audience?

* * * * * * *

Of one thing I am certain: Human nature has not changed.

In every language, most people take pleasure in verse, by which I mean carefully chosen language that is rhythmic, fluid, clever, apt, and which conveys ideas and stories that seem important and truthful.

Let me break that definition into its parts:

Carefully chosen language
rhythmic
fluid
clever
apt
Conveying ideas and stories
important
truthful

This definition of verse does not try to distinguish between "high" and "low" poetry, or even "beautiful" or "powerful" or "edgy" or "cool" or "classic."

Instead it describes what people look for in verse. Some will be better satisfied with one poem, others by another. What you call "good" poetry may differ from my list. But what makes it satisfying, *as verse*, are these attributes of both language and content.

Love him or hate him, there can be no doubt that Byron is writing verse:

> My heart is sad, my hopes are gone,
> My blood runs coldly through my breast;
> And when I perish, thou alone
> Wilt sigh above my place of rest.

But the same is just as true of the much-criticized Edgar Guest:

> Bring all the wanderers home to the nest,
> Let me sit down with the ones I love best,
> Hear the old voices still ringin' with song,
> See the old faces unblemished by wrong,
> See the old table with all of its chairs
> An' I'll put soul in my Thanksgivin' prayers.

Yet even though these poets were much beloved and widely read in their day, both of them—and all these verses—are in virtual oblivion today.

The poetry itself is unchanged. It is easily accessible to modern readers.

What has changed?

* * * * * * *

There is some truth in all the speculations I offered at the beginning of this foreword.

Technology. Recorded music often trumps printed poetry for the very good reason that music has its own power, and while the lyrics of songs are definitely verse, they are at the service of the music (and vice versa).

Also, recordings freeze forever a particular performance, with flaws removed (as much as possible). When the performance really is excellent, it often leaves amateur efforts looking pale and sad by comparison. And every time we read a poem to ourselves—especially when we read it for the first time!—our performance of the verse, though usually silent, is almost always amateurish. But, being human, we blame the poem, rather than the reader.

Education. When I was a kid (in the then-excellent California school system), I was given poetry from the start—and had to memorize it and recite it aloud, which is essential to learning to love poetry.

When we were assigned to write poetry, it was English metrical forms we were taught—that is, we were taught to take part in our own culture. Yes, we were given a shot at haiku, but it was a brief portion of a much longer exposure to traditional English-language verse forms. We learned our iambic and anapestic, our tetrameter and pentameter, our ballad stanza and our sonnet and our heroic couplets.

By ninth grade, our teachers expected us to recognize these things when we saw them...and we did.

My own children had no such training. But then, they hardly had training in anything. They would have been as ignorant of history as of poetry, if we had left their education up to the schools.

Demographics. Poetry is most passionately received at a certain age—fifteen to twenty-five, usually. That was also, not coincidentally, the age of Byron, Keats, and Shelley during most of their careers as poets.

In their day, literacy was widespread—but book-buying wasn't. A poet could be considered "all the rage" but still be read by only a small portion of the whole English-speaking population.

* * * * * * *

But it is a mistake to suggest that modern poets still appeal to the same small percentage of the public as ever.

Books are cheap today, comparatively speaking, and libraries are plentiful. Money and illiteracy are no longer a barrier. Yet those who read a book a year are still only a fraction of the 15-and-older audience. So we have indeed sorted ourselves into a literate audience and a larger public that don't have much interest in books.

Out of the *reading public*, what percentage are aware of contemporary poets? I believe that any rational estimate would recognize that the percentage of devoted readers who voluntarily read *any* new poetry is vanishingly small.

Nor can the lack of poetic education or the competition with pop musicians explain the decline in the audience for poetry. Because the hunger for verse is unabated, and people *will* find poetry, if it is offered at all.

Else how can we explain why, in the 1960s, the poetry books of Rod McKuen became bestsellers—despite the howls of the college professors and reviewers? At exactly the same time the Beatles were at their peak of popularity, here were these poetry books, popping up in the hands of fifteen-to-twenty-five-year-olds.

Who are Rod McKuen's successors? Rap performers, of course. Yes, I'm a sophisticated enough reader to know that as verse, rap is usually pretty awful stuff; and its popularity is usually explained away as a fad of "rebellious youth."

But I think that people, especially young people, *will* have their verse, as long as it seems important and true to them, and is offered in language that is *speaking to them*.

* * * * * * *

In the January 2005 issue of *Poetry*, the best and also most accessible of the literary journals being published today, editor Christian Wiman introduced a section of essays about poetry by non-poets with a short essay that began with these paragraphs:

> "Louis Menand...defines the beginning of a profession as the moment when practitioners of a discipline are no longer answerable to those outside of their field, but only to their peers. Such a devel-

opment has obvious advantages for fields like astronomy and medicine, which involve complicated and advancing bodies of knowledge, and which depend for their advancement upon the exclusion of amateurs and quacks. For poetry, though, which doesn't 'advance,' and the best of which is sometimes *written* by amateurs and quacks, to become professionalized is a disaster.

"But that is largely what has happened in this country. Not only has a clear 'career path' developed for young poets, who often spend their entire poetic lives around universities, but the whole enterprise often seems to have high walls around it. Poets determine what gets published. Poets review other poets. Poets give each other prizes. To be sure, there is a lot of life and energy in the small, professional country that is contemporary poetry. But for those of us on the inside, it can become all too easy to cultivate and reward an ambition that does not extend beyond its borders." (*Poetry* 185:4, p. 300.)

The walls that Wiman writes of are entirely of poets' own construction. For a good while, the public was beating on the walls, or walking around and around them, looking for some gateway, some window, some secret passage that would let them in.

* * * * * * *

What do those walls consist of?

I should write a hundred pages on the history of those walls, but not here. I will merely summarize: T. S. Eliot and Ezra Pound shaped their inevitable revolution against the previous generation of poets by writing allusive, elusive, elitist poems that demanded, not mere hearing, but study.

Their imitators, in order to create the illusion of depth, removed surface meaning from their poetry.

Their revolution would have been a positive thing if it had been followed, in its turn, by an anti-elitist, romantic, "people's" move-ment, for pendulums do their work only when they swing back and forth.

Unfortunately, two things happened to poetry:

First, universities began teaching contemporary literature, and they adopted the principles and the canon of "modernism" as time-less laws and timeless works. So the fashion of that day became a wall of stone; individual poets might fall in and out of fashion, but college students were invariably taught to value only the kind of po-etry that not only *can* be decoded, but *must* be decoded in order to have any meaning at all.

For those who studied that kind of poetry, the great works could be quite rewarding; but the general public tried to read it and felt stupid, looked-down-on, left out. As well they should—that was precisely the result Eliot and Pound intended.

Second, when a feeble attempt at a revolution happened in the 1950s, it consisted of the Beat Poets, whose "poetry" amounted to little more than a formless screech—or, to cling to the simile, graffiti on the same stone wall. If you happened to be Leftist and angry and contemptuous of bourgeois values, the graffiti might give a bit of a burn, but for the rest of us, there was neither poetry nor fire in it, and they did nothing to open up the wall.

Indeed, as they became embraced and co-opted by the academic elite, their rejection of traditional values became part of the wall, another way to keep the ordinary people who still believed in those values outside the citadel.

* * * * * * *

There are other lessons that young would-be poets learn in uni-versity. I remember a friend of mine in grad school at the University of Utah who said, "You have to find a *region* to write about. I'm going to be a Southwestern Poet." I was stunned by the sheer cyni-cism of it. Not that he wasn't qualified—he *was* from Arizona, and a talented writer. I simply had never thought of a poet choosing his subject matter based upon a desire to further a *career*.

But...didn't Shakespeare write love sonnets because there was an audience eager for them? Didn't he write epic poems because that's what would give a young writer a respectable reputation?

Ah, but here's the difference: Shakespeare still wrote so as to include as many people as possible within his poetry. In the search for the apt wording that fit the poetic form, his syntax sometimes knotted up a bit and required some decoding—but not much, and the audience still recognized, instantly, the importance and truth of what he was talking about.

You can't recognize what's important and true in a poem if you have no idea what's being said.

* * * * * * *

Perhaps just as important, however, is the rejection of form. Eliot and Pound had mastered traditional forms before departing from them. But their imitators (and the imitators of their imitators) have not bothered to take that preliminary step. Most modern poetry falls leaden on the ear. They sneer at the "doggerel" of Edgar Guest, but are incapable of matching his mastery of form and aptness of phrase.

* * * * * * *

The walls surrounding poetry today are high and thick...but they are not, in fact, stone.

An audience still hungers for verse that is powerful, true, that is rhythmic, fluid, clever, and apt. And there are poets who never succumbed to the university nonsense—even though many of them won university degrees.

I remember, many years ago, sitting in a hotel room in Dublin, where a young reporter was interviewing me for an Irish magazine. It came up that he was also a rapper. (He did not say "poet.") I asked to hear a rap, and he recited to me.

It was, first of all, very good poetry. He didn't know it, but he was writing in tetrameter couplets with a bit of sprung rhythm; because he regarded "poetry" as something done by lofty professors, he had no idea that he was reinventing forms that they had largely stopped praising, but which once ruled the English language.

His language was beautiful; his narrative was moving; it was poetry. He had to call it "rap," but he still wrote it and memorized it and recited it aloud, the way real poets do.

I read the cordel poetry of a Brazilian poet (and friend), Braulio Tavares, and was profoundly moved by the realization that there were still great talents in this world who had no wall between them and the untrained reader. Tavares understood and understands that if your verse resonates with the ordinary person, the elitists, who are always late to the party of literature, will follow afterward.

A few years later, I saw the movie *Il Postino* and immediately bought a collection of Pablo Neruda's poetry. Because I read Spanish, I bought a side-by-side translation and what stunned me in reading it was that Neruda apparently hadn't heard that poetry was supposed to be obscure. His work was beautiful *and* open. There was no wall. I realized that only English-language poets are sneered at for writing to the common people.

* * * * * * *

Now, after all these pages, I come back to Michael Collings's poetry. For he is the artistic brother of Pablo Neruda, Braulio Tavares, and that Irish rapper whose name is sunk deep in some cold pool of memory.

Therefore he is also the brother of Byron, Keats, and Shelley.

His poems are difficult only when the most apt way to say a true and important thing requires a bit of unraveling to receive it.

But always his intent is to tear down walls.

Collings's poetry is a path, a road, sometimes even a highway, taking you to destinations you did not even know you wanted to visit, and yet you always did in some deep place in your heart, and when he takes you there, you recognize it and realize that you are, for this moment, home.

When the Dreamer of Worlds Awakes

Dusk. A solitary world bows its
Crystal face toward blank stars. Fires huddle
Heat unto themselves. A smooth arc swings,
Unseeing, past an azure-tinted moon…
And the Dreamer, worn with labor, sleeps
    into a desert waste where
    heat
    defines all unseen boundaries, where
    heat
    squats chafing on streaked brows of leathered men
    leathered women   leathered neutrals
    sexless   genderless   naked to the
    heat
    that swells thickened knots of pain
    lashes flesh   tears flesh
    desiccates flesh and leaves behind
    just husks…,
    except where angry hearts store
    hidden treasure, cooling treasure, liquid treasure
    to transform their world; and in the roiling moistness
    of their hoard the
Dreamer's flesh prickles with unwanted heat,
The Dreamer's sensate skin grows damp and slick,
The Dreamer's sleeping eyes demand sweet dreams
    of water everywhere,
    fathomless, silent, except its constant
    hiss

water upon water
infinite within the bounds of this small place;
water swirling currents without name
through eons without name
fingering evolving life
without names
small flitting forms
breathe their magic
build fragment empires
where resistless currents
hiss
beneath enormous emptiness that
Startles—the Dreamer almost wakes, then sinks
To unseen depths that marshal close against
the darkness of a dying sun,
dying breath that rouges dying sky
raises dusty pillars with
anguished cries of fear and pain
and horror—
feels a rush of sudden hope
swirling
Deeper into darkness, the Dreamer whirls
world upon dizzying world,
possibilities multiplied upon themselves—
uncountable scarlet leaves
swirled kaleidoscopic, mythic storms—
until
(like grains of sand
washed cutting-sharp by ages)
each silhouettes
into the Dreamer's self
becomes the Dreamer's self
amplifies the Dreamer's self in
galaxies' spin-frantic magnitudes until
The Dreamer wakes, rises, walks into
The light…to generate infinities,
To organize vast worlds without end

SCIENCE FICTION

I Wander the Cosmos, Inventing It

> "I wander the island, inventing it,"
> —Robert Coover

I wander the cosmos, inventing it,
Punctuating petty galaxies and venting wit
On ochre shades across the face of cockade suns.

I step where I have stepped before
In prescient Fancy—because I step there
It now is there beneath my foot.

I wisp bleak solar winds to kites
With planetoids as tumbling tales for ballast—
And stutter mumbled mirth at clumsy comet-heads.

I wander the cosmos, inventing it,
Perpetuating physics as an odd-time afterthought
To fill the void my passing makes.

I gender entities with facile breath
And, disabused, come splattering my way
Between green distant lanes of not-yet to-be stars.

I think a purple groan of sand beneath
A thousand tons of oily shale, beside a fractured
Fossil shell. I think a solar system's eccentric planes.

I wander the cosmos, inventing it
And in an instant of slant prospective
Loiter longingly on a micule coil

To spin it…whirl it blue and hominid
In orbit around a —*there it blooms now!*—
Gelded sun. I think of *me* and generate

Me paper poem reader—fit
audience and few for this imagining….
Then—wandering—move on through nothingness.

BECAUSE I WOULD NOT STOP FOR DEATH

Because I would not stop for Death,
Death tried to stop for me;
She placed her hand upon the land—
She touched the fevered sea.

She harvested vast fields of souls—
She struck this Earth with blight;
I hurried past the blasted stalks—
I tuned my fear to flight.

She tried to hold me back; she offered
Entropy and calm—
She curved her hands to scimitar blades,
She touched my nerveless palms.

* * * * *

I fled to paths between dark stars,
To curves that bisect space—
She followed me, the Lady Death,
And strove to win the race.

In tandem, Death and I pursued
Spin-wheeling galaxies;
We raced at light's velocity—
We took what we might seize

Of time and space and curvature—
We passed the speed of light
And entered a new Universe
Of Death—of Me—of Night.

* * * * *

And still we raved with frantic pace—
Attenuated life—
We passed all bounds of consciousness—
Became our mindless strife....

Mere moments have passed, and æons died—
Since I've begun to see
My Death and I are lock-embraced
Toward Infinity.

THE LAST PASTORAL

*TO THE READER: "The Last Pastoral" contains language and situations
that some might find uncomfortable to read.*

Come live with me and be my love,
And we will all the pleasures prove
Damn Marlowe! And his pastoral!
Damn them both to bleakest hell

while I sit here, listening
to that damned tape-deck malfunctioning,
squawking an incessant tape
of Renaissance poetry.
                        Whatever ape

programmed that should be shot!
No...the bastard's already got
his reward, along with.... Damn
them all! This red button would ram

a warhead down their throats, if they
had throats again. They don't. I play
that incessant, insane, sing-song voice
for noise, you see. I have no choice

Since Newman died. The bastard! Leaving
me alone like this. "Grieving
for Earth," he said he was. Like hell!
For a ball of shit that might as well

blow itself to bits, explode
like a scarlet weed, unload
enough energy to bring
us home a million times.
                              Sing

damn you! *Come live with me* Or die
like Newman. Hell, I didn't lie
to him, or seduce him while
we were drunk that night.
                              I'll

admit that we were bombed—bad pun,
I know—we were drunk, then...none
too sober, not sober enough
to want to see that dirty scuff

that hid the stars, dirty smudges
of a planet that turned its fucking grudges
on itself...yeah, we were drunk,
two breathing bodies cased in a hunk

of metal on an airless moon.
We talked, and cried, and cursed, and soon—
oh what the bloody hell!—we touched,
broke some convention much

more honored in the breach than valid
for two dead men in the pallid
ash light of dead earth. *If all
the world and love were young* like gall,

or salt in slashes, the taped mewed
piously. And we were nude,
bodies alive and warm where had been
only death before.

And truth in

every shepherd's tongue.
                                                    I took
him. When we woke, he looked
at me. He stood there naked, bare
and skinny, silent. He bled stale air

into the lock and stared at me.
And cried, damn him! He cried. To see
his face like the ruined earth
gashed with lines, giving birth

to death.... He smiled—once—to mock
me, walked into the lock,
sealed the hatch, and decompressed
himself. His blood
                         But could youth last

and love still breed
                              and blood still bleed,
exploding like a scarlet weed
against grey steel. *Had joys no date,*
nor age no need His bloody hate

abandoned me! But I can get
him...I'll show 'em, teach 'em yet
to fuck with me, to shoot me
into empty space
                         If we

had worlds enough
                              and leave me here
alone *and time and time* They'll fear
me. Damn that tape! *time*
This coyness laddie were no crime

were no shut it off! *crime*
no crime My warhead's poised, primed,
aimed. I'll blast the earth to bits...
no, I can't...it's gone. Hit

the button anyway! Maybe
Deserts of vast eternitie
the fucker'll short-circuit, explode
itself like a scarlet weed, unload

its flames.... Newman! Where's he gone?
Get in here, you shit—don't leave me alone!
Then these delights my mind might move
To live with thee and be

NOTE: *"The Last Pastoral" received a first-ballot nomination for the 1986 Nebula Award—Short Fiction Category; and second place for the 1986 Rhysling Award—Long Poem Category. It also has the unique distinction of being the one of the only classically formed pastorals yet translated in its entirely into Klingon, along with explanatory notes by the translator, Robyn Stewart (see APPENDIX).*

THE BONEYARD OF OLD EZRA SNOW

For Robert W. Service, Roland Mills,
and memories of Campfires many years past
(with apologies to Orson Scott Card)

I

Oh, the galloping stars can shoot by like bars
On a chromascope's L*E*D scales;
And the vacuums of space can dilationally race
Like runaway carts on greased rails;

Oh, I've shot like a spark through vast cauldrons of dark;
And I've skimmed suns and come back alive—
But the worst thing I've seen was a swatch of Earth-green
In the Boneyard on Tiâmat Five.

It isn't a boneyard displayed on an Ad-Card—
At least, not in the regular sense;
The corpses don't pile for mile upon mile,
The headstones aren't crowded and dense.

No, on all of that planet (should future scouts scan it)
The body-count's set at "dead-low"—
From East clear to West, on that whole world there rests
Just the dry husk of old Ezra Snow.

Now old Ezra Snow was as small as they go,
And his puniness stuck in his craw;

If one hair had been shed from the crown of his head,
He'd've missed the base height set by law.

But Ez, he was scrappy—that old boy was happy
To take on six men twice his size;
And he gained a rough grace in weightless, dead space…
And on Tiâmat Five—dead—he lies.

II

Now, our worktour began with a random name-scan
When the Comp'ny computer decreed
That old Ez and I were prime meat to try
To find Class-M planets to seed.

(*Class-M,* that's the label that means that we're able
To transform a desolate planet;
Though if we glean data from life-bearing strata,
The Company's ordered to ban it!)

But back to my story—…old Ez in his glory
Had set up a miniature station
With everything cut down, from console to shut-down,
And all built with three-quarters steel rations.

Then he scuttled inside as if planning to hide
Or to sleep until Sol's globe burned pink;
For subjective weeks I got nary a peek
Of old Ez—just his voice on the 'link.

But then came the day when he crawled out to stay,
All sweating and burned up inside.
I did all I could, but it wasn't much good—
In four days and two hours, he died.

When he knew it was time, he put hand to mine
And pulled 'til we touched, face to face;

With fingers like claws, and his throat fever-raw,
He whispered, "Remember!—not space!"

Oh, who would have thought, when drunk on a pot
Of imported Rigellian wine
And we uttered an oath blood-binding on both…
That the proof of the pact would be mine.

Should one of us die, the other would try—
And try *to the death!*, was our vow—
To *bury* the other, and goddam the bother,
On a planet…somewhere and somehow.

And now Ez was dying, and I would be lying
If I said that I wasn't disturbed;
He gripped my hand tighter—that scrappy old fighter—
And made me again pledge my word.

Then he rolled back his head like it was made of pure lead,
His claw-hand fell limp at his side;
His heart gave a hitch that meant, "Life's a bitch!"—
And old Ezra quit breathing and died.

In cold space the dead do not lie in a bed,
All painted for mourners to grieve—
But I made Ez a casket from a cargo-hold basket
And drank to his lost *joie de vivre.*

It set my flesh creeping to have Ezra sleeping,
A corpsicle stored in the hold;
I'd turn up my collar and unthinkingly holler
For old Ezra—but he lay stone cold.

In a month I arrived at Tiâmat Five—
Class-T, so I knew that no missions
Would labor below and disturb Ezra Snow
In his timeless and death-darkened visions.

I scanned the world's surface, found a spot for my purpose,
Then landed and worked my fell chore—
I scooped out a hole by a thin sapling's bole
And laid Ez there for time evermore.

III

O, the spaceways are wide, and since Ezra had died
Two years had flown by…almost three.
When T-5's smooth bight hove into my sight,
Well, I just had to stop there to see.

I landed at night and was thus the spared the sight
That startled my eyes at next dawn.
For acres around, the rock-studded ground
Lay dead grey—all the saplings were gone,

Except in the middle (a great, living riddle)
Stood a stories-high, bright Earth-green tree;
With branches swept low, where the dawn breeze would blow—
And I swear they were whispering to me!

I crept a bit nearer and hoped to hear clearer
The frustrating, murmured derision—
For I knew in my heart that I'd played a main part
In this mystery haunting my vision.

"Hey, Jake, is that you," the leaves whispered through
An alien, sand-colored glow—
"Is it you come back here, to grin and to leer
In the boneyard of old Ezra Snow?"

I took a deep breath that tasted like death
And strode to the giant tree's trunk;
I placed my palm flat on its bark, gave a pat
Like to say "I don't take any bunk."

But the whispering came like a murmur of fame,
Soft at first, but growing in strength:
"Disbelieve if you will, but my friend, this is still
Old Ez—live in timber and length."

I must have passed out; when I roused, looked about
At a landscape sharp, alien, and skewed,
My head pulsed with pain—but that voice fell like rain
From sick skies: "Now, I don't blame you!

"You couldn't have known, when you buried my bones,
"What this world was able to do
"With cryo-chilled cells and DNA wells
"Of raw protein—no, I don't blame you!"

I started to mutter some stupid, weak stutter,
Base words meant to stave off cold fear,
But the branches bent lower and laced in a bower,
And their murmurs imprisoned my ear:

"When I first felt called back from the comfortless black
"Of the grave—from the depths of Death's sea—
"I panicked in pain and dared not hope to strain
"To this height—Oh! the height of a tree!

"I first felt warm light that shattered my night,
"Then moisture and soft, palming wind…,
"And at once was aware of this sun's heat on bare
"Branches thin-pinioned and blind…."

There was more stuff like that—a comfy chit-chat
With some bark and some leaves weirdly painted—
But when one branch got bolder and twined on my shoulder,
I yelped…and I jumped…and I fainted!

This time I came to more slowly. The view
Had subtly altered, had changed.

The tree still stood there in a spot nearly bare,
Its Earth-green still eerie and strange.

But the lattice-work wall that had once seemed to fall
All around me was gone—I lay sleeping.
The breezes whirled high—huge clouds scudded by—
And I heard the soft rhythms of weeping.

"Ez? Ezra Snow? Can you hear me?" But no—no
More voices answered my call;
But the vivid green swirls, the skyscraping whirls
Of green branches stretched proudly and tall.

And I knew without doubt that old Ez was about—
That his spirit…his cells…or his genes
Were not just alive on Tiâmat Five—
But *flourishing* like nothing I'd seen.

And the weeping I'd heard—like the song of a bird
In bright branches at midday in fall—
Was the weeping of joy from a short, dead ol' boy
Now tall, taller…tallest of all!

I stepped back a pace to give myself space
And scanned that tree crown to trunk;
I cocked my head square into the still air,
And said, "It's nothing but bunk!

"There's no way in space that the ashes this place
"Once greeted could sprout into this!"
I stepped close again and fingered the grain
Of bark that suddenly hissed!

"It's me, curse you, Jake—and make no mistake—
"It's me just as sure as you breathe;
"And I'll tell you this, lad, be you good or plain bad,
"I'll be growing long after you leave!"

I could take it no more—I raced to the floor
Of the lander and lying there, panting,
Slapped the stud with dispatch that would close the space-hatch—
And I left that weird planet of haunting.

IV

Now the galloping stars still shoot by like bars
On a chromascope's L*E*D scales;
And the vacuums of space dilationally race
Like runaway carts on greased rails;

And I still shoot my spark through vast cauldrons of dark;
And still skim suns and come back alive—
But the best thing I've seen is that swatch of Earth-green
In the Boneyard on Tiâmat Five

THE PROGRAM

For W. Gregory Stewart and "Robo-Ben"

Once upon a workshift dreary, while I programmed, bleak and
    bleary,
Stationed at the hard-drive terminal just inside my cubicle door,
While I plodded, nearly napping, there rose a fearful, whirring
    clacking,
A sound like demons gleefully wracking, racking as in days of yore;
"It's just a glitch," I softly muttered, "just a glitch in the memory
    core;
                    Only that, and nothing more."

Ah, distinctly I remember how, like a distant fading ember,
My server-file refused to send or call my cursor to the fore;
I lost the file I had created, my monitor grew dim and faded,
The malignant-eyed computer made a dismal sputter, just before
It spat one time, then blinked, and then resumed as it had been be-
    fore.
                    It *was* a glitch, and nothing more.

Or so it seemed. But when I called the file I had assiduously hauled
From planetfall to planetfall, defining my parameters for
The requisite restructuring of cells, of blood, of functioning
Anatomy for landfall cloning, cloning tissues as they were;
Then, then!—my God!—the empty spaces that glowed where *I* had
    been before!
                    Only that…and nothing more.

And then I saw the program shifting, each backlit column clearly
    lifting
External data, clearly sifting through the sentient options. Nor,
With that content, terminating its random matches, random matings
Of gene with gene, recalibrating tissue textures that I wore—
Recalculating planes and tissues in the body that I wore—
                            Changing forms… and something more.

Squint-eyed, peering at the data, poring through white-static strata,
I struggled not to estimate a shape my spirit would abhor;
My fingertips…despairing, flying…praying that the file was lying,
I punched the program, deeply sighing for the peace I'd known be-
    fore;
"Let it be a disk-drive error," I whispered, damp in every pore:
                        The cursor spelled out: *"Nevermore!"*

I stared at the configuration, at the bitnet simulation
Of the imminent manifestation planned for me by the memory core;
I saw the horrid, pallid features of the craven, driven creature,
Of that rhymester over-reacher resurrected from before—
I saw his haunted features and the look of madness that he bore:
                        "Not that!" I pleaded, "nevermore!"

But the program, never veering, kept revising and repairing
Until I saw his visage peering red-eyed with its gimlet gore—
"I do not want this verbal horror! I do not want to mourn Lenore or
Ulalume, or spend my furor in this rhyming, pounding roar!
Re-program me!" I cried—demanded!—and fainted against the cu-
    bicle door
                    When the cursor spelled out: *"Nevermore!"*

                    * * * * *

And now I've lived through three more missions, felt my atoms
    twist and fission,
Found myself in this position, huddled over a computer core—
Three times I've found myself a craven coward seeking for a haven,

Surcease from that metric Raven that pounds within me o'er and
    o'er—
From this ranting, chanting versing, from this meter I abhor:
                                    Quoth the program: "Nevermore."

So I wear his black mustaches; so I dream that I may slash his
Image…pray that I can crash this program's jingling, jangling
    core—
So I sit with fingers curling on the keyboard, data swirling,
All my energies unfurling to make me as I was before.
Done! Press *Enter!* That should do it! Make me as I was before!
                                But the screen gloats, "Nevermore."

RETROGRADATION

For Brian W. Aldiss

"And time run back and fetch the Age of Gold."
                                    —John Milton

"…what we regard as the flow of time in fact moves in the opposite direction to its apparent one…. Energy accumulates from less organised to more highly organised bodies: piles of rust can integrate into iron rods."—Brian W. Aldiss, *Cryptozoic!*

Immortal Christ twines through Eastern twilight,
Enters the Cave of Birth. Cold flesh

Waits solemn agony, bloody birth upon the Cross,
Remembered through futurity to Adam's time.

Three days dwindle…Friday sunrise…Spirit
Invests waiting flesh. Long-shattered

Legs knit whole. Blood spurts puscid blindness from
A soldier's eye…ascends a stark wooden shaft to

Thrust warmth into the Christ's pale, heaving breast and
Whole a splintered heart. Time-made-Mortal slowly

Moves to trial, betrayal's pain, glory, wondering
Discipleship—arriving duskily to peaceful

Death in a stable-stall…God-child
Returns into his mother and unto his God.

Eons wander—humankind assembles.
Demons sweltering in outer Hell surge into

Heaven, gradually forget rebellious thoughts
Until Christ and Lucifer confront—and Lucifer,

Restored. At the End, all children of the great immortal
God gather unto Him, Eternal and Unchanging. The plan

Fulfilled. Creation gathered at the foot of
God—and none are lost, and none are left behind.

SUCH THINGS AS WORLDS

I shall touch one page today—solid humdrum
dust that someone one-time said our Dreams
were made of—touch…there…real beneath whorled,
callused fingertips. It required a full
year's salary, this BOOK. God knows how it
meandered through the galaxies to rest
in our poor port, but it did. Without thought
I bought it—honest paper, warped cloth
boards four centuries old at least…maybe
more. The stuff of dreams—*words…words* on paper…
thin, dust-fragile sheets that might flake away
with touch. I touch one finally, today.

Tomorrow, I shall turn that page, lave
my soul in WORDS—such things as worlds are made of….

THE GALACTIC AMBASSADOR Is Invited to Hear the Hand-built Organ on a Newly Conquered World, Its Function Explained by the Victorious PLANETARY OVERLORD....

...a rarity, I know, on such
A world to find an instrument this pure,
Hear sounds as wide as russet skies. Oh, much
Harsh labor was expended, as I'm sure
You understand. The lowest pitches fell
In inaccessible marshes; the mid-
Range flute-like tones, from living stasis shells—
We must re-voice them when the shells are dead.
The highest songs—Ah! those notes that break my
Soul and wring rich tears. Our masterworks! They
Are digits, hollowed with the dying cry
Of barely sentient creatures from the bay....
    But speech diminishes...a grey disease...
    And you, too, weep to share such Harmonies.

RENASCENCE

Mathema*tic*
>   *tick*
>   *ticks* a cosmic time-
piece:
> CopernicusBraheKeplerGalileoNewton
>   time-
bombs primed:
>   *tick*
>   *tic*
mathema*tics* overturn a universe of
crystal spheres
>   (fragile evanescences of eternity
>   spinning in mythic harmony)
dissolved in acidic enlightenment
and
mitish man swept—spinning, mewling mote—beneath
>   straw*ticks*
>   *tick*
> mathema*tic*-ing center-Earth
into a finite speck:

into the vacuum of exploded space

INVERT LOGIC

What senses do we lack that we cannot see or
hear another world all around us.
> —Frank Herbert, *Dune*

1. Antithesis
What fool! In errant, blinding madness, he
Senses 'others' we whole ones cannot see.

2. Thesis
"Do they think this world fallow just for us, that
We—guided to this Garden-grove where lies no
Lack of Earth-growth greenery—
That we again are offered simple Paradise?
We conquered Space—one day shall conquer Time—but we
Cannot surmount inherent ego-centeredness. We refuse to
See strange shapes through other-facet eyes;
Or touch beyond direct impingement, nerve to flesh;
Hear the *thrumm* of alien pulse.
                              There...just under sight,
Another quiver of not-light in heartbeat with this
World...unseen sound perceived through touch or taste; yet
All they hope is to recover our self-immolated Earth."

3. Thesis Confirmed
Around the nestling ship, a glimmer-shimmer draws
Us cloistered—malleable atoms in shaved crystal claws.

ORION DISAPPEARED LAST NIGHT

For Algis Budrys

Orion disappeared last night—
or rather, disappeared some light years past
and only seems to us but lately gone,
to join the other starbelt clusters

flaking off.
Where it was—component stars and
vast vacuity…an emptiness
that shatters hearts imprisoned here

on Earth. Tomorrow night…the next?
A month? Who knows—except Orion
too is gone, a fragment flake of universal
styrofoam peeled away beneath

A cosmic Thumb.

COLONY

Before I left, he called to me. My father
Touched my hand, my head, and spoke his death
That must occur while I explored vast youth-filled space.
His eyes grew dark. Dim starshine kindled light

That flowed on metal fins, a fluid light.
And I, pinioned in an embrace that, father-
Like, enclosed me from the poisonous womb of space,
Slept centuries, my sleep a dreamless death.

When I awoke, I felt as though cold death
Had speared my heart...until *my* planet's light
Reflected azure-opal through black space:
An other-Earth where life could bloom. My father—

Long swathed in death—reached and spoke. My father,
Living in my memory, circumvented death
And crossed the centuries of sterile space
To touch my head and bless me for that light.

He blessed me, my dead father, in his death,
Swept me through space to this world's breathing light.

ELEGY FOR AN ASTEROID MINER
DYING ON DECEMBER 25

Christmas means little to me here,
Deathtrapped in this pit where ammoniac
Snow piles centuries above,
Loneliness looms centuries wide throughout a
Metal-sheathed, artificial coffinwomb.

Metal gearbeats nearly drown out squawking
Christmas disc-tapes that patter-echo into
Loneliness where dark dreams glow and
Death smells ever sweeter in the guttering air—a
Snowfall of forgetfulness.

Snow-static crinkles as I try to speak beyond the
Metal of my gravedeep world—I only hear
Death rustling nearer as a wind...and
Christmas fades to dreams beyond all
Loneliness and fear and cold.

Loneliness...a-loneliness…no...
Snow of hydrox-crystals does not make
Christmas, nor does the fact of mindless
Metal lungs outpouring poisoned
Death scant breaths away invalidate its claim.

Death comes. I cannot halt its flow. But
Loneliness...I reach through acid air, beyond my
Metal bounds. I wait to die...and they touch me.
Snow-flake coldness numbs my cheeks...frantic
Christmas lights escort me home again.

SPATIO-TEMPORAL SPECTACLES

I went with him this afternoon
to pick up his first pair,
and watched his adolescent
cockiness

evaporate behind new inch-thick
syntho-lenses and curving bio-bows.
His organo-eyes grew larger,
deeper midnight blue,

and when we walked
he walked a curious, high-stepped
walk, aware that—soon—galaxies
could gape beneath his feet.

And I was back
some thirty years ago
to my first pair,
and walking home,

my own feet weaving
a curious high-stepped walk
as chasms yawned just beyond
my sight and my control.

Even then, I knew the plasteel walk
was level. Until I fully activated them,

I was in no danger of a temporal plunge.
But every step became an act of faith

that road was solid road
and drops that opened up
beneath the orbit of those circled lenses
existed only in my mind.

I made it home—and so will he.
And after several days my eyes
adjusted to new foci, to new range,
and all the universe was mine.

Imagined chasms closed....
But never again was it so easy
to believe that roads are solid roads,
that time is time is time, and

that those half envisioned chasms
did not
never will
exist.

Note: "Spatio-Temporal Spectacles was a Rhysling Award—Best Poem finalist, 1994.

HESPERIOS

For M. Shayne Bell

I cannot breathe   for Venus
low in black black night   over
comes me in her passionnet
emblast of blacklack light   en

shrouds darknestled nightmere fares
fallingfailingfiling   sharp
end honing wholly angles
sole daughter of the west   to

me she hovers nightbright star
ing succubus   inhaling
earthbreath thru nosthrills mor
tal forefate to her brightbreasts

CONFUTATIS

dying Mozart beats the time beats time
itself thunder-voices echo and re-
echo dying Mozart's timelessness
in a braincase

doomed and dying thundering its voices
time to time in time with distant
cycles of a sun not his not mine
a death we share

in frantic waste his time my time shuddering
in collision with an alien moon de-
scending for the last time lending
a silver sheen

to his fever mine i did not want to come did
not choose this deafened world of dark-
ness of despair alone except thoughts
and Mozart's death

music confounding ears lost to earthwaves
ears hammering thick air screaming
release against thick air clotting lungs
that belong else-

where elsetime elseworld i would hear once
more pounding voices voices light
as starflecks on seeking eyes i would
hear his death song

LOVE AMONG THE STARS

Naked under alien stars the man
and woman breathed, embraced. Colony's rule
forbade such things, of course, but—oh—how can
reason govern need? Forbidding was fuel
for mounting flames. They stole away beneath
two dawning moons, threading blue tendril vines
that, rampant, wound and clutched. Earth-loss, green-grief
fled far from them. Caresses first, quick lines
traced by eager fingertips—cheek, neck, throat,
breast, thigh. Traced. Retreated. Returned. A dark
flush boiled in bursting blood...earth-lust afloat
on stumbling ecstasy...sigh-breath...then...sleep...;
while twining plant-things puncture, smother, kill...,
join one to one in lost-lush other-still.

WHEN THE CONQUERORS CAME

And when the conquerors came
From space and blanched our land
With withering flame
And iron hand,
We cried in vain to the conquered gods of old.

With alien form and alien mind
They twisted life across
Their ways. We pined,
Rebelled, and lost—
And cursed in vain the conquered gods of old.

Our remnant tribes dispersed by night
To mingle memories and tales—
The legends grew in might,
Drew cries and hails,
Re-built in vain our conquered gods of old.

Though scattered, tribal remnants knit
A loose combine of rugged strength—
Slack-muscled arms grew fit;
Dire weapons grew in length
Of fire to flame our conquered gods of old.

* * * * *

Some died...the young, the strong, the fit. The ill
Stood sentry till their fevers flared

And burned their sight—then blind, they filled
Their self-appointed stare
Toward the light of conquered gods of old.

Some lived...scorched limbs knotted in torturing pain,
And wished to die but choose to live, to fight
With weapon, brain...with blood—to gain
An inch, a yard, a hillside height
Once sacred to the conquered gods of old.

At first the conquerors held, withstood the push
Of focused arms. They stood...then faltered, asked
The worth of this small globe—the bloodstained blush
That stigmatized their thankless task
Now fired with power our conquered gods of old.

* * * * *

Then swelled a dawn when alien ships afire
Reversed the heavens, withdrew their fevered crews.
There seemed no cause: the conquerors' deadly ire
Had simply died. With relief our soldiery withdrew
To think upon dead, conquered gods of old...
To worship now the conquering gods of old.

ALIEN METAMORPHOSIS

Spring came overnight. Pseudo-snow
drifted rocket-high, transformed itself
to shoots of Earth-growth green (a pleasing hue
for human eyes), of metal-red, of delft

clad with copper over-sheen. Plants spurted
visibly, leached silicon nutriments
from saffron soil. In hours, the camp lay skirted
in rainbow fringe. Then arching vines formed tents

above the colonists...and withered, stilled
as death itself, an Other-death. One man,
a botanist, pressed a switch too soon, killed
the force field, and stepped out. The dead began

to live again, to scent new creatures' breath,
and wrap them all in twists of hungry death.

EVOLUTION

They laughed. The last surviving lungs
drew poisoned air, and they laughed...
barked...coughed like criminals just hung.

Already he felt hollow, and she felt cell graft
to cell, capture and enfold and engulf and
cling—drowning bodies on red-corpuscle rafts

swirling within her bloodstream. Hand
in figurative hand they smiled and stepped
from alien into sanctuary lands.

EXILE ON A LEFT-HAND WORLD

On this world we redraw our mental maps,
Since its ungainly orbit laps its sun
In obverse motions from the one we fled—

And more. Its breath tints vision red. Its mass
Tugs traitor flesh as if to signal danger.
Our steps press strangers' feet to alien folds.

This blur, this weight will surely pass.

Its lifeforms boldly insinuate odd shapes
That subtly ape earth-vision matrix modes:
Pale jellid nodes that mimic sentient ways.

Our reticence will fade one day. Perhaps.

Its continents, its bays of viscid foam,
Its frothy loam where Earth seeds half-mutated
Spike spindly oblate stalks of gaseous green.

All this may soon be redefined as home.

But this world preens its mottled amber face,
Then turns away—rotates in counter motion—
West to East its oceans' wrinkles flow.

There is an insidious wrongness to this place.

We do not *know* the twist. We cannot see—
We only feel, intuit counter surges:
A world's too large a vastness for our eyes.

We do not *know* it…consciously.

But still Wests rise to Easts. This world's floods curl
In converse furls that draw *our* lifeblood rhythms
Backward with them—backward through our hearts.

This is not a human-succoring world.

Contortion darts like lampreys on our souls,
Distorts our poles and arcs and latitudes
Where human pulses will not, cannot adjust—

For this new earth, we must draw new mental maps,
Since its eccentric orbit laps its sun
In obverse motion from the cinder-cone we fled.

A Lesson in Manners

"Don't dawdle," he said, "it's not polite;
we always walk a brisk, quick pace.
Don't keep gawking here all night;
and whatever you do, don't show your face.

"You're frightening—you know you are!—
to those of my gentler, lovelier kind.
You're a backward creature of a moribund star;
don't, I repeat, keep falling behind!

"And I wish you wouldn't glare so mistrusting.
I'm only going to show you to folks
who still don't believe in life forms disgusting
as you. Straighten up, you biological joke!"

He leveled a kick at the native pup,
who politely smiled...and ate him quite up.

MY DOG IS SITTING IN A TREE:
AN ALIEN VILLANELLE

My dog is sitting in a tree—
In my mind, I see him fall.
This is not the world for me.

It's not a dog, of course. You see,
Here all things fly, not creep or crawl,
So my *dog* is sitting in a tree,

Although, you know, it's not a *tree*.
Not really—nothing's as it seems at all.
This is not the world for me.

This earth is like an air-blown sea,
And, like an eight-winged crystal ball,
My *dog* is sitting in a tree.

Perhaps in words I've found a key—
Words to build an image-wall.
But this is not the world for me.

I'll name it *dog*, I'll name it *tree,*
Pretend they're what I choose to call:
So, my dog is sitting in a tree....
No, this is not the world for me.

ABORIGINALS' ESCAPE

silent
they

suffuse cold molecules
microscopic debris accumulated from decaying, alien husks
fog-plankton and clouds of disembodied scales
sand and stone and shell and sea

silently
spread within the captive bay
spread and glow upon the wrinkled face of commerce-clotted waters
spread and glow and glimmer broad arcs beneath dark, hulking hills

glimmer, glow, and focus upward
spin specks of light that call an unseen watcher's touch—
startled starward they invest
become

a
moon

Spiral Galaxy [I]

whirl of cochineal
shrunken-head pinprick light
invisible to eyes that strain

beyond heavy atmosphere
beyond vibrant dreams of generations

vastly ponderously wheeling
star-studded twist-swirl
universe to alien infinities

Spiral Galaxy [II]

beyond heavy atmosphere
beyond vibrant dreams of generations
invisible to eyes that strain

shrunken-head pinprick light
star-studded twist-swirl

universe to alien infinities
vastly ponderously wheeling
whirl of cochineal

INVENTING A GALAXY

inventing a galaxy
i sketch, consider
(*con-siderare,* 'to observe
the stars'—of course,
how else to build
a galaxy), estimate

what stitches
physics requires
to arc each spiral ray
gracefully
around central emptiness
(*black hole*, symbolized
by nothingness)—inventing

a galaxy—blocking
colors, textures,
shapes, sizes…,
constructing mental blueprints,
stars beyond
conception

Fine threadwork for a protoGod

FAR ACROSS THE GALAXY,

carved into a stone temple,
mirrored by pollution
lines crawl in weathered hieroglyphs

bones gnarled with silicates
molder in translucent
air—sulky, beetling contagion

artist's legacy almost
erased—millennia
of poisoned exhalation-dews

still, carved in stone, an image—
monstrous and alien,
bipedal, erect, and deadly

THE MISSIONARY'S RETURN

It was the best two years
I've ever spent—
Two years (subjective time) in preaching
To distant peoples,
Living as one with them in distant lands.

It is a joy
To stand before you to report,
And see my family
Assembled here.

Grandsons and great-grandsons
Of my Brothers
Administer the covenants
As always, without change.
Their Sisters sing in sweet concord
Those hymns I knew before I left,
Holding antique hymnals with gentle force.

In front, my Mother and my Father
In holograph
Smile and nod as if they were alive,
As if their eldest had not traveled
Half a hundred lightyears
At just below the speed of light
To preach the Gospel of their Lord.

I would bear my testimony
In that language that I served,
In that language that I love,
If I but could—
But microsurgery to restore
My throat to human speech
Closed off those sounds…
As my mission has closed off
Memories of who I was,
And I am left a stranger
In a different world.

But I am content.
My mission was a grand success.
We baptized many,
And that suffices me
For all things I have lost.
*If called again to go
I would not hesitate.*

THE LEGEND OF KOMETES

By the shores of urPangaea
By the swampland where they labored—
Where they bred, great thunder-Masters,
Where they hunted, tyrant-Masters,
Where they wandered, roof-plate-Masters,
Duckbilled Masters, armored-Masters—
By the swampland shores they wandered,
Wandered herds of massive Masters.
Loud their footsteps where they plodded,
Loud their breathings, loud their crashings
Through the greening under-forest,
Loud the air of urPangaea,
Echoing their potent cries.

Came the Long-Hair slaying day-light
Came the Long-Hair killer stalking,
Stalking through the blue of heaven
Stalking through bright day of night,
Making nighttime burn as daytime,
Turning nighttime on the Masters.
Came the Long-Hair, seeking, slaying,
Slaying Masters with its breath.

Forests burned and forests blistered;
Swamplands died in hissing pain;
Meadows scorched within an instant,
In an instant-life of fire.
Heat-sail-Masters shriveled, screaming,

Screaming fury as they perished;
Winging-darters tumbled earthward,
Earthward shrieking, wings aflame;
Thunder-Masters thundered faster,
Thunder-plodded as they fled;
Tyrant-Masters ceased their hunting,
Ceased to seize with awful jaws
Flying, fleeing, scurrying masters—
All consumed in Long-Hair's blaze.

Still the Long-Hair stalked its victims,
Slaked its thirst in victims' blood—
Mighty Masters fell in moments,
Died in moments where they fell,
Flesh engulfed by Long-Hair's fury,
Flesh now blackened, crisped and sere.
Still the Long-Hair sought destruction,
Worked destruction on the slaves,
Humble slaves of Thunder-Masters,
Humble, hairless, fingered servants
Cowering in deep shadowed caves.

Long-Hair died amid its flamings,
Died as forests, meadows died;
Long-Hair burned and slaughtered Masters
Slaughtered Masters, forests, seas.
Then came darkness, chilling darkness,
Darkness at the height of noon.
Darkness cloaking starry heroes,
Darkness hiding rampant moons;
Darkness chilling servants, darkness
Leeching color from the skies.
Plants grew paler, spindly, whitened—
Paler as the darkness grew .
Long-Hair's children—ice and winter—
Made their nests in Masters' bones.
And the servants, humble servants,

Humble, hairless, fingered servants
Waited in deep shadowed caverns,
Waited, waited for their spring to come.

FIFTH MOVEMENT...AND FINAL
Symphony in E-Minor "From the New Worlds"
[Organ Transcription]
Second Recension

sound shudders   console cramps beneath twisted
barbs   molten flesh fencing with pinioned flutes—
mourning doves stutter ruddy lines of fate
cathedral/calm   storm-fires rubyFires through
stone/lattice   ruby-shivered-glass shards stone-
bone floors
                    I play
                         GhostChoir antiphonies
nave/birth/death at one   I   orchestrating
darkness   bloodLight oozes on thick ivory

sound shudders   organ weeps ultimate mu-
sic penultimate.
                    I the last
                              surge bile-
black/captive notes   beyond whiteAsh gray/Loom-
ing wreak/wreck/wrack world   petulant defile
Fifth Movement   SynSymphony uncomposed...
Climax thrusting into deepest *oneliness*

10^{33}

years from now, when the final proton
sighs and dies into black nothingness, when
      ["*the executioner's sword descending with languid grace*"]
only electron and positron survive
of all the forms the Big Bang gave

form to, when attenuated particles managed
by magnetic fields and foraging

through infinity spare lightyears distant
from each other agree with full consent
           ["'*vaster than empires, and more slow*'"]
to constitute an Entity,
when time and space slow to full eternity...,

...,

Entity—galactic-huge, sentient inorganic
thought incapable of peace or panic
           ["*wispy magnetic consorts*"]
decides (over a century of archaic years)
to move a spiral arm through ghosts of stars,

sweep meditatively across remnant-memories
of chemistry and physics and cosmology,

disturb its subatomic particles a fraction
of a parsec, and with that inarticulated action,
      ["*to the slow thumping of the universal heart*"]

move appendage a minimal, millennial nod,
and contemplates imagining a god.

[Quoting Gregory Benford's "Introduction" to *Far Futures*]

StarSong

StarSong echoes the endless
 Songs of God
   Brilliant Biting in
    December nights
   Softly blushed in June

StarSong weaves uncounted
 Worlds Webs universes
   into Harmony-Breath
    of God made
   Shimmering Flesh/Flash

StarSong threads itself
 expands contracts
   Cosmic
    Sand-dollar
   Sand-dart's tapering spine

StarSong winds the Speed of
 Light in knotted hanks
   conjoins Planet-Orbit
    Sun-Flight
   spiraled Galaxies' rotundity

StarSong blushes
    Brilliance Sings
        wings and waves and sines and
            warriors to
    God

MoonMasks

MoonMasks shelter pendant
    Worlds from infinite
        Darknesses of pinpoint
    Stars ineffable and lit
    against the lightless pit

of night. Floating MoonMasks gently
    wash pitch skies
        with repeated, amply
    varied blurs of whites
    and greys, shadowed lights

encircling Earth. MoonMasks approach,
    oppose gravities—
        lunarchic coaches
    joining cosmic levity
    to material solidity

and, masked, reveal deeper blazes
    beyond sky-dark,
        behind star-ghost lasers—
    MoonMasks mock
    Fear...and sheen dull, earthly rock.

StarHeart

Shard blackness in flame
Shred infinite silence with screams....
Atom to atom wrenched
Nuclei dissevered, expanded, exploded and

Holocaust visits outer realms
Gas clouds and dust swirls that imitate
Galactic nebula until

StarHeart bursts in sweeping gouts
Of stellar blood
Shed in expiation for its inner fires
Its gravity beyond all weight and time

BLACK HOLE

Midnight Rose, dark bloom
swallowing vestige light and hue,

collecting in great sweeping swirls,
swirling frantic furls of Color-Space;

tighter, tighter, until all components
compress—a shrinking ball of blackness…

smaller than figment
nothingness.

Dark bloom, midnight rose—
red to purple, purple-black; rust-mote

collapsed beyond sheer sight
beyond sensation—gravity

compelling even
light; Imprisoned

Time serves
dark Eternity

COSMOLOGY

I cannot help it.

I see Wanderers and Long-Tailed Stars,
Not planets, comets.

Orion is for me a jewel of ice-locked light,
Not hot and distant suns.

Scorpio curves brilliant venom
Across the marges of my mind.

The moon waxes, wanes, breathes saffron-silver warmth,
Alive, not dead.

I study, define, compute, manipulate—
And still I cannot see objective stars.

CELESTIAL DANCE

We are the wanderers, shifting stars
That hold no single place but sway
In sure rotation, point to point,
Step and counter-step, until
Deep music swells, climaxes, falls....

We are the long-haired travelers,
Smooth scimitars of light that slice
Through shell and solstice, bisect others'
Neatly circled orbit-spins,
Swift cynosure of envy's eyes.

We are the galaxy, flowing milk,
Pure path across the cosmic night,
Enlightening with each arcing swirl,
Each whirling pearl, each silken curve,
Outshining sun and lucent moon.

We are the heavens, the bowing skies,
The universe, the single-turn
Transforming dance to elegance—
We meet at passion's molten core,
Transcend infinity with our kiss.

It's Long Past Tune-Up Time Again

I went today to get my head
examined—it's been acting up lately,

starting sluggishly, idling roughly,
braking at the oddest moments, when I would think

that it should rev. So today, I bowed
to the inevitability, sat down, and called the head

mechanic down at Mike's Place,
made an appointment for just past

noon, and went on in. He opened
up the skull, clucked once, and peered inside—even

invited me to watch if I cared to
(I declined, read month-old magazines

in his waiting room instead). "Well,"
he announced an hour later, to me and to the

waiting room in general, "That should do it.
I've tightened a few loose bolts, caught a squeak

or two that might be giving trouble,
oiled everything that moves and polished those

that don't. It's running smooth now,
smooth as silk, I'd say. Should keep on running

for a long while if you take care—change
those ideas frequently, take it out on the freeway

every now and then, blow the dust from those
dark corners, and don't forget that the more it sets

idle, the rougher it runs." I thanked Mike,
paid the bill (reasonable, it seemed to me) and left,

surprised at how painless it had been and
how much I had missed without knowing it the silent

humming of a well-tuned
head

SCIFI-KU

Evolving proto-amphibians
    crest, blink, breathe
        new possibilities

Within my computer-self...
    generating alienselves and
    silken moons

Stuttering 'holo-screen
    reveals intensity—
        silver souls beneath

Ice-world snow unmelted
    for 10,000 years—
        Lover's-heart incised

Pearl parings stain
    apricot tapestry—
        new moons' suns-set arcs

100-square-mile
Sail billows…. Hydrogen breathes us
Toward Infinity

Orbiting satellite—
Electron to our sublunar
Complex nucleus

Before galaxies,
Planets, systems, suns, and gods—
Camellia soul blooms

A rocket cuts through
thick, dark air, sears infection—
a flaming scalpel.

Star-rise in the south—
sequins stitched on the fabric
of unknown star-scapes

I become aware
of wide imagination—
I look up…no stars

From the Moonbridge arch,
A silver moon curves slowly
Through gilt majapads;
The azure moon casts five-armed
Shadows over crystal waves.

And I wait in my
Ice caves, as silver-missile
Flames consume my world;
The four-limbed conquerors shall
Shatter, fragile in their heat

MYTH AND FANTASY

THE PASSING OF ARTHUR: AN EPYLLION

I.

Glowing shrouds whisper trailing flames,
Swirl grey triple masts in scarlet dusk.
Sorrow-laden, bearing low its bier
Dark-swathed, a bark sets out upon smooth swells,
Pearlescent swells, toward the lonely isle
Of Avalon; three gentle queens, a bier
Whereon the wounded king reclines in pain,
And a somber shadow-hull fades into dusk.
Men stand in silence on rock-bound shores;
As truth fades into hope, hope into fear
An emptiness descends upon scoured sands
Exposed by egging waves gravely calm;
Deep in silence stand the stone-still forms
Bathed in saffron fires of passing day,
Remembering...remembering the past.

Days of glory, halcyon brotherhood,
Visions of the Cup of Holiness,
Great carven chairs about the Table Round
Where none held precedence save Arthur King;
Days of greatness, courtesy, and truth
Forever riven now through treachery,
Through subtlety and guile.

                    Where now the Crowns
Which jeweled mortal brows? Where now the shields,

Deep-burnished coats of fire-forged mail, bright swords
Inset with sparkling stones and scarlet gold
Once wielded by mighty champions,
Now pitted in the lifeless fist of death?
Where now the emerald serpent, that which caused
The bloody fray? That asp whose fangs were bared
But never struck? for Modred's knights rushed on,
Arthur's knights stayed not but joined in war;
And Arthur's mail-clad heel—unknown to him
As he in mortal warfare flashed a brand
Renowned above all lesser, duller blades,
Warding with his massy arm sharp blows
Upon his chalice-helm, his breast—
Bore down upon the adder's deadly skull
With crushing might. Where now the bonds of trust
Uniting knight and legal sovereignty?
Fading toward twilight Avalon.

II.

Not far away the mirrored mere lies calm,
Unmoved beneath cool, crystal-starry light;
And in the deep unruffled depths soft-green
A warming golden glow quiescent lies,
Suffusing all in aureate majesty;
The Lady waits in rapt solemnity,
The jeweled pommel of Excalibur
Upon her samite gown—the Lady waits.

III.

As dawn first spreads across the Lake
The Saxon yeoman ambles stolidly
Toward the furrowed sod, his seedless plot;
And as he leans upon a hand-hewn hoe,
The harsh bright light of day subdues the lake.

A VISITATION OF GRACE

I sit one day
to read,
cradling the volume

until a subtle itch emerges
beneath my scapula,
behind my heart.

I shrug against my chair, twist
absently, cross
hand over shoulder, reach

vainly.
Subtlety distends, distracts.
It—*obsessing*—mounts

and a secret presence velvets flesh
and soothes.
Ahhh! yes, there...that spot...

enough...
enough!

Enough! I cry, and
the shadow volume slips to the floor.
No more!

Still claws curve
through graying emerald scales
ripping mercifully

my dragonhide.
Painpleasure, pleasurepain, pleasure only
mounting into joy.

New-naked, quivering,
heart-exposed,
I bow to reach the book,

Crossing into Narnia
where *Aslan* is the King.

"Stretched Naked on His Bed, a Second Danaë"

A second Danaë, stretched naked on his bed,
Ransom lay, a random sacrifice,
A golden shower glittering on his head,

His mind obsessed with what he had long read
Of Space: vacuity, revealed as Paradise
To Danaë, stretched naked on her bed

As Zeus appeared. Life standing in the stead
Of exile and of death. It would suffice,
That golden shower glittering on her head.

Just so Ransom—Earth-born, Earth-bound, led
Against his will through human cowardice,
A second Danaë. Stretched naked on his bed,

In awe, one with the vastness, almost wed
To stars disclosed by one bent man's device,
A golden shower glittering on his head.

He discovers in the void Great Light—not dead
Empty space, but Arbol's living hospice:
A second Danaë, stretched naked on his bed,
A golden shower glittering on his head.

Note: The title quotes C. S. Lewis' fantasy, Out of the Silent Planet. *The poem received a Rhysling Nomination, Best Short Poem, 1983, from the Science Fiction Poetry Association.*

THE SURVIVORS TO THEIR HEIRS:
A QUOTELLA

The final night collapsed upon the earth;
Sun faltered; plenty counterfeited dearth.

Shall that endure? No! never while we can
Turn a hand to soil or penetrate
The unknown depths of stone. Never while the
Color of noon-sky remains in mass
Of memory, or sound of sea, breaking on
A granite cliff. Never while pock-mark craters
Bruise the landscape; or a single shattered wall,
Its broken teeth a vile curse, lay like a
Giant cancer on the murmuring ridge.
Black has not won. Dark has no victory;
Deceit and treachery shall taste defeat,
Shall fall, retreat at last before our dawn.

Be sure of this: the Dark, though mad with mirth,
Swollen with gore, shall fear your valor's worth.

Roc

Wide wings, football-field wide,
Knotted with jets like seedpods
Swelling with cancers. Grey hide
Glisters sunlight above clouds,

Above air almost, before
It swoops morning-bright wings wide,
Drooping beneath the ice-grey door
Of dawn, to drop a single

Torpedo egg to earth.
Then up again on updrafts
Self-generated. And birth
Of death hatches bursts behind.

MEDUSA

sulfurous serpents
chlorine cobras
coil concrete
cornices   flicking tongues
twisting fangs
to steely skies

around her head twine
sinuous threadhaze
venom spatters mirrors
scores aluminum
abrades glass
lest some Perseus attempt
to slay
by reflection

stone grimaces
watch their approach   chill
as scales scratch
granite and lime   corrode
saints gryphons gargoyles
reduce earthbone stone
to blackened
ash

EURYDICE

"Eurydice, see Orpheus"
—The Oxford Companion to English Literature

Sing of Phrygian Orpheus...lightly,
    as other singers' voices have.

Sing his god-doomed love and struggle
    with the serpent's bitter sting;

Sing his slow descent into Avernus
    to confront Death's iron smile;

Sing his painful, wrenching laboring upward
    toward day's looming birth;

Sing his too-soon turning, one fatal step
    too near the orifice of gloom!

Sing his sorrowed wanderings, songless grief...
    death pregnant with disembodied melodies stillborn

but not to me! who faded in the dusk
    beneath hell's curling lip
    and felt my woman's song too throbbing
    to be sung

MYRMIDON

Mindless scuttlers over sun-seared soil,
yeanling warriors waiting to deploy,
rewarded with red-gold for their bloody toil
marching against the might of Troy;
insectile, formic, millipedic swarmers,
doomed to death by Achilles' vaunting pride;
onslaught of caustic potency, heedless stormers,
never halting till Troy's vaulted walls subside.

RESTRICTIONS

From the painting by John H. Pitre, 1972

Bellerophon perhaps—in a world
where more than one Pegasus
mounts varnished clouds—strains
against the coiled tendrils that
vine-like wrap his wrist.
                    Pegasus himself—
wild-eyed,   wings   pinioned,
twisted, torn and tethered—arcs
his neck and mane in one tense
thrust against an arid waste that
holds him slave.
                    Bellerophon rides almost
naked, his arm outstretched to
clouds, his fingers outstretched
taut, to grasp the vision of another.
His naked thighs press into his
Pegasus; his naked foot curves
around his mount's outstretched
leg. His naked broken sword lies
fractured on heat-fractured, end-
less, imprisoning everness.

Bellerophon perhaps—in a world
where more than one
Pegasus mounts vanished skies
—strains against tight shining coils
and struggles to unfurl his nascent wings

SABRINA

In pure chalcedony, opal-edged and swirled
    as winter leaves on nearly frozen streams;
In pure chalcedony, milk-blue and toil-curled
    as frozen tears on amber-russet beams;

In angelite, in crystalline celestite born
    of Tethys, rivers' mother, delicate
In blue of froth and foam, Sabrina's songs adorn
    bank and leaf-strewn bed, ever rustling.

In willow wands Sabrina twists her liquid locks;
    in sedges swooning on the river's shore
She waits and watches. As the shepherd wards his flocks,
    Sabrina breathes her presence on the flood.

HORROR

…Is Death

Dreams brought me to this catacomb—
Dank necropolis breathing heavy rot
Through sable soil moldering with age.

Dreams unspeakable—drawn from ancient tomes,
Dark whisperings—brought me here. I wait, caught
Between sleep and madness—in this close cage.

All around they rise, creatures of the gloom,
Twisted, tortured, skeletal—they rise from plots
Of creviced marble, fingers crooked with rage.

In dim-light, pale bones gleam like polished chrome,
Ragged cerecloths counterfeit hangman's knots—
Fell accoutrements aching for a stage.

They shamble, scuff beneath an arcing dome
Of root-clogged earth, haunted by worms and clots
Of new-dead flesh, corruption's equipage.

I back into a ravaged, crumbled combe,
Hope to hide from their contempt, their quick hot
Gasps of hatred, their murderous rampage.

In dream, this fearful darkness felt like home,
Familiar, comforting—yet now, distraught,
I feel it smothering, black doom's presage.

Closer—they surge across bedeviled loam—
I shudder, scream— my tears avail me naught—
My cursed dreams gape…I've earned their deathly wage—

THE DWELLER ON THE EDGE OF DAY

Between light and dark, in twilit
Afterglow, of neither day
Nor night but shunned by each—

Afraid of night, of sunlight slit
Into portal dreams that prey
On stuttered, sullen speech;

Afraid of day, too numb to pit
Rampant light against the sway
Of midnight's selfish reach;

But caught, unwilling to submit
To either, lest one betray
My bleakest fears, impeach

This half-life nothingness as fit
For neither breath nor death, flay
Consciousness to screech,

A wail, an agony—commit
Me to damnable decay,
Beyond all healing reach,
Beyond all saving reach.

"Night's Plutonian Shore"

"Tell me what thy lordly name is…"
—Edgar Allan Poe, "The Raven"

Some say the way is Stygian dark,
Cerberic, fraught with harms,
Phlegethonic, its wild flames stark,
Impervious to spoken charms,
Impregnable to arms.

They tell of wells of bleak dismay
Assaulting pilgrims' souls,
Of horrors waiting to betray,
Demand their fill of terror's tolls
Like gnarled, vicious trolls.

But worse—the curse of nival ways,
Of palely vapid streams,
Hung low with heavy-frosted bays
Where woad and madder—ghastly gleams—
Choke paths to darker dreams;

Where ash-streams clash with frozen stones;
Where melancholy dwells;
Where time-lost souls proceed with groans
To hidden, nightmare-ridden cells,
To endure prodigious hells.

IN THE HOUSE BEYOND THE FIELD

Cold beyond white fields it stands,
Empty, lone, outlined
With grey, landscape winter-bland,
Blind façade unlined
By twisted, dead ivy strands.

White-framed, shuttered windows stare
Blankly at bare trees;
All about, a distant air—
Neglect, loose debris
Fluttered in an icy glare.

But inside…inside, where dark
Shadows roam in rooms
Abandoned to waiting, stark
Emptiness, shapes loom—
Unfocused, horror's birthmarks:

Beneath raw floorboards a heart
Beats judgment, throbs guilt;
Behind a bricked wall, apart,
Aslant, quickly built,
Moans cascade with subtle art;

In one room, undead wails rise
From thick, black, sealed vaults;
In one, cats' ungodly cries
Screech without a halt;
In one, a raven looms, flies….

In a dead man's mind, a flask
Of wine spills, parches;
Room to room in solemn Masque
Death softly marches—
Ghosts resume bloodcurdling tasks.

THE HAUNTED VALLEY

The iron-green of juniper (black
Beneath the crescent moon, shadowed remnant
Of the day) foams silent, adamant,
On rounded hills. Misting breath, raised hackles

On my neck, goose-flesh freckling arms
In spite of down-filled-jacket warmth, I grapple
With raw fears. The wrecked stone chapel
Where I was cursed looms—splintered door ajar—

Ghost-like in this sin-mulched vale, symbolic
Of the limbo where my soul now stands,
Tangible reminder of the brand
That mars those born in this false-bucolic

Place. My flawed blood throbs with torrid blame,
Pulsing permutations on my shame.

BLACK CROCUSES

Black crocuses beyond mold-
crusted graveyard gates. Petals prise
wintered breath—shriveled petals, old
beyond knowing, curse wintered skies

from stony ground unhallowed,
unconsecrated. They unfurl
blackness beneath scattered, shallow
ashes spurned by winds that swirl

beyond the wall as if propelled
by the dark one who lies unBuried,
perhaps unDead, whose will impelled
individual molecules carried

on vagrant air, that even yet
pervade black crocuses, twine
downward in unknowable nets
where waits, impatiently, to dine,

to surfeit on web-wrapped parts—
the crimson spider at their heart.

It Waits for Me

It waits for me,
winged shadow
in clefts of wailing ash

that overhang dark
barren fields,
thin furrow-graves for leaves;

It waits for me,
eyes yellow as
bright sunlight glancing upon stone

wings dark as midnight
moon glittering
on a silvered bow;

It sometimes
speaks its harsh
crude mocking cries

and sings faint
whispers of
its knotty sheen,

sings hoarse
minuets
to my waking dream

But ever it
waits for me
waits patiently for me

in darkened
clefts of wailing,
failing, trailing gray-green ash

VIGIL

I cast myself upon her grave,
Fevered brow on hirsute ferns
Like fringed tiers of lavender.
                              I rave
And dig necrotic fingers
                    into midnight earth

Black with sullen tears. The moon
Glows red, a baleful, mocking maddening
Urn for hopes of bliss. But wait!
                              The grave
Gapes—I'm borne through Death
                    into the Womb of Earth

Where she awaits with scarlet eyes
And scarlet teeth and scarlet lips
To draw me in. I sleep…her willing,
                              living slave,
My head upon her unStaked breast,
                    In blackened, unDead Earth

THE GRAVE

December's flood-tides haunt the ghostly plain,
Echo silvered sheets across flat dark.
Roiled waters lap long grass where I have lain

And grieved my father in his mossy park.
By moonlight, when wild storm-flood flows
And catches with its verge the stenciled mark

Of gravestone, there I wait. Carrion crows
Circle widely past the moon, dip, and wing
To darkness once again. Endless rows

Of graves lie breathless beneath the flood. A ring
Like liquid silver marks the drowning place—
And as I stare aghast, the flood-knives sting

The willful grass and knot it in their grasp. My face
Reflects against dim moonlight and full flood—
Black waters surge and swirl their deadly race

To beat each other, moil through grass and earth and mud
And reach with pale-stripped fluid-bones into dark depths
And draw him forth…a finger joint…a blood-

Cloaked clot of shoulderblade…a skull bereft
Of flesh. Eye sockets rock beneath the waves
Of gaunt December storms. They search to right, to left…

They pinion me, and seem to speak. The grave's
Become a sinkhole choked with mire—my father lies
Denuded, broken, staring like a slave

To evil fortune through two black eyeless eyes.
Thunder cracks somewhere beyond; lightning gleams
And shatters from his rotted teeth. Lies

Slither serpentine across the filth. Lies told,
Unspoken, shared across lifetime's rack of pain.
Mud cakes my palms and knees. I shiver with the cold.

December's flood-tides haunt the ghastly plain,
Echo silvered sheets across the dark.
Roiled waters lap long grass where I have lain
And grieved my father, wrapped only in my cloak of pain.

GREY

A scintillance of grey sparrows
spears an old black yew pruned in tough
       triangular grace

beside black asphalt on a grey
November day—splintering ash
       and charcoal as they

flick the yew with pinions poised, re-
verse, reverse, reverse until grey
       blanches white and flat-

sheening feathered mirrors flock grey
clouds, grey sun, grey dying day one
       final burst of light

A scintillance of grey sparrows
sparrows-not-sparrows but UnDead
       others calling night

CONTAGION

Still in the womb he twists
shoulder-high
murmuring secret thoughts
of future breath,
of blood pulsing free, his
own pulse, of half-formed
breast smoothed
with muscled flesh to
bear his waiting
heart toward
another
rest

She waits, face hooded
with shadows of
the past,
with unwanted shades of
future fears—
she feels him twist,
feels unborn flesh bite against
her flesh
and cradles rue
within her waiting,
wasted
arms

VAMPIRE

A vampire lives on the old homestead,
shadowing deep attic corners,
darkness in the light.

It lives there still—
but once it was threatened, I think,
when the Valley banded together

and built the new-brick church
on the corpse of the old-stone chapel
a generation old.

For a breath, it hesitated,
paled, faded into shadows cut in stone
above wheat fields thick with rattlesnakes.

For a breath...then it remembered:
water rights...arguments...disfellowships...
mindless faith that led

to numbness, stultifying
death.
And it returned to prey

as always on the living blood,
to suck hearts dry
that should have lived deep pools,

roiled among the shadows,
emerged with glittering and thirsty fangs

VISITOR BY STARLIGHT

It's less than a rustle in my ear—
An instant of black where night should be.
A sensing of something drawing near.

A fragment of heart-beat stilled, then free;
A flicker of shadow behind the moon.
The moment I tense…it's stalking me.

A flush-heat of blood; a molten boon;
A sheening of death-chilled ice on skin;
I know that he's coming…coming…soon.

A flutter of breath allows him in,
Grants him permission, the will to dare;
My needs battle terror…needs must win.

My eyes seek the wall, my neck-line bare.
My bed is my coffin, my hope, my bier;
I feel him beside me, translucent air:

It's less than a pain, a hiss, a fear;
A sheer hunger sated; a crimson tear.

THE WANDERING UNDEAD

The moon skims low across night skies;
Pale stars abrade silk clouds;
Stark night rests dark on glade and park;
Black yew trees twist unbowed.

> *The night has fed*
> *On daylight fled;*
> *It is the time of madness and*
> *The wandering UnDead.*

Their fœtid breath on window sill
Recalls me to wild fears—
My shrouded lamplight dies to night,
Bitter as unshed tears.

> *I lie abed*
> *With horror new-bred—*
> *It is the hour of madness and*
> *The wandering UnDead.*

They pass my opened, unchained door;
In ghostly garb they walk,
Grey-shrouded forms that whisper harms,
From room to room they stalk—

> *They fill my head*
> *With murmured dread—*
> *It is the time of madness and*
> *The wandering UnDead.*

From stone-cleft haunted catacombs
They echo banshee wails,
They poison ears with acid fears....
I feel my heartthrob fail:

> *Dry eyes burn red,*
> *Harsh breathing fled—*
> *It is the hour of madness and*
> *The wandering UnDead.*

Their hissing bursts frail bonds of life—
I rise...I stand...I faint—
My fingers clasp their ice-fleshed grasp—
My lungs freeze with constraint.

> *No more abed*
> *I, too, am led—*
> *It is the time of madness—and I join*
> *The wandering UnDead.*

AFTER FIRST BLOODING:
REVISITING THE VAMPIRE'S HAUNT

In the vacances of years, where shadows spawn
Dust-rustles in dead tarns of memory,
In blackened spaces beneath raw, ancient eaves
She moves—thin spectre self—and moving, breathes

Isolation and voiceless lust. I seek her.
My lamplight slices darkness with unsubtle gleam,
And pinions shades, and—illuminating—slays
The form that is now my constant memory.

Enlightening, light passes. When I can see
Clear edges on dusty attic furniture
Or rafters heavy-hung with harmless webs
Beneath crooked fingers of light…no mystery.

For that brief flash, no blood; mute peace and rest.
But lamplight fades and vision's sharpness fails,
Crisp edges infold to possibilities….
Again—*o gods*—she hovers at my throat,

In the vacances of years, where shadows spawn.

BEFORE THE THROAT IN NAKEDNESS

brittle dust-dry flesh
coffin-carrion
wrinkled parchment map of mottled years

slashed ravaged bare skull
taut cheek-bones
flaying bare-skin gaunt ash-grey

hag-killing eyes—black-on-
white-hunger gnawing
fifty years of unfed dagger-lust

grey-on-grey tight lips
hip-bone bowl
unhuman nightmare fey-skeletal

rust bone-blood-brain
rope-thin sinews
binding bone to undead thirst

before the feeding
before it rises—bends
before the throat in nakedness....

SOLILOQUY IN ONYX

Darkness dulls the senses, kills
their feeble wills—
entraps them in futile dreams,
muffles faint screams
that otherwise might warn them.
Night will condemn
them to vacant, groundless fears,
while blood-bright tears
shimmer in my moonlight, lead me
to night's dire fee:
arced heads, vulnerable veins
for me to drain—
hot blood spurting on pale sheets,
temptingly sweet—
life dwindling under my kiss,
eternal bliss
passing lips to waiting throat,
gracile as motes
of dust on unfurling wings
while midnight sings.

AT MIDNIGHT

She watched the night-news re-cap,
Last gasping cable from LA,
Watched the channel
Fade to angry starstorm static.
The video place had upped its price that day—
Five-fifty for a first-run film,
And she was too incensed by the blatant rip-off
 (It was the only rental outlet in this burg)
To waste her money there.

So she sat and smoked and drank and stared
At nothingness enfleshed in patterns on
Fake-oak paneling in the rented room.
The static grew insistently.

She stretched, she let her nubbly robe
Drift open, and the snow of breasts
And waist and thighs
Matched flurries on the set
That coalesced, extruded, blended
With the dark-oak backdrop,
And he stood cloaked and silent—then
With a whisper, naked by her knees,
And she leaned back and smoked and stared
At watermarks that marred hypnotic
Cartographies of cheap ceiling tiles.
She bared her eager throat.

Once she moaned and bit her lip.
Once she cried.

At dawn she woke. Exhausted. Sore.
Bloody. Depleted fullness and
Dampened fears. The channel flickered
Its test pattern, giving birth to some
Charlatan selling ginsu knives or cars,
She did not know or care which one.

LAMIA

Child-stealer, child-killer,
Monster-mother murdering night—
Mask-faced mother robbing cradles,
Vengeance stinging
Desiccated
Lips.

Semen-stealer, semen-sipper,
Phantom-lover shod in night;
Love's death-pale phantom-lover,
Stealing manhood,
Stalking youth-fulled purling vigor
In despair.

Blood-bathed, breast-bared,
Serpent-bodied kiss of death—
Lifeless, deathless, death in life—
Shimmer through pale moonlit shadows,
Hover
Other mothers' sons.

2:30 A.

2:30 A.
M. and full
and blood-
ed Lord
of Dark-
ness roils
ebony
walls

dreaming
UnSleeper hot
and fervid
UnDreams
flesh
and
blood
and blood
and Blood and
Flesh
beyond cold
tendril grasp

He roils
full and
blood-
ed plunges
darkness into
Dark-

ness shatters
ebony
silence
with UnSpoken
lusts

that
he
himself

does not
fully know

Lord of Darkness
full and
blooded
UnDead
bringer of
Death
and his
body
urges pro-
creation

(BLOODED STAKE
SEARCHING HIS
BLACK HEART)

even in
his
black-
est
dead
UnDreams

THE DAMNATION OF THE DAWN:
A VICTIM'S AUBE*

Cruel sun! too soon, too soon you slither
amber glass, rose-dusted sills, then down
thick red-blood carpeting. He turns
in sleep—my lover turns—and through thin walls,
my other clumsily begins dull morning rituals.

Officious warden of unending day—
He does not guess…would not believe it if he could.
But still…. A knife-edged sunray slices
sheening quilt, caressing bed and sated flesh
with hideous warmth. And my lover moans.

* * * * *

Again! lonely in anemic dawn,
condemned to share a daylight bed
with the old one creaking wearily beyond the wall.
Sunlight, higher now, cuts ebony coverlets
wrinkled in flat mockery of his form—

A shadow weds deeper shadows in
hidden cornices. Deadly sunlight blooms
blood-red on my waxen fingertips—
I weep pale, tasteless blood…and silent,
sullen emptiness mocks me from my bed.

Aube: a rigidly defined morning poem. The speaker must be the woman in a love triangle, who expresses regret that dawn is coming and that she and her lover must part.

THE VAMPIRE'S DAYMARE

Bright-blood swirls through lips again, whorling darkly
In nubs of tendril-tongue, splashed in worn-away
Spatters on pale, uncallused, unDead palms.
Sleep is murdered now anew, pungent sleep
Where *my* hot blood can roil in peace.
Sleep dies—and haunted red-rimed eyes
Confront dark light, dark blood
Benighted memories
Of shrieks, cries,
Screams of pain—
Knife-blood release—
And steaming gouts
Of dankly
Crimson
Blood—

INCHANTATION

i invoke the blood and
flesh invoke the blood and
bone invoke the blood and
spirit soul housed
in blood and bone

i revoke the thought re-
pent *pensée* penitent-
iary imprisoning blood and
bone imprisoning blood and
flesh

i evoke the god
the god and embryo and
flesh and flesh and flesh that curls
entwins gives birth invokes more
blood and blood and blood

A Visit from Grandma

When Grandma comes, I grab my hat;
My Grandma, you see, is a vampire bat.
She creeps and skulks in human form
All day long, and tries to warn
Me of the dangers of the sun,
And banister-rails, and all things fun.
She hovers over my every move
And never bothers to reprove
By word, but thumps my aching head
And spanks until my cheeks glow red.
But if Grandma by the day is horrid,
Grandma by night is a phantasm borrowed
From nightmare fears. When evening falls,
She shrivels to dust and, with wild howls,
Discorporates to a wispy mist.
Next thing I know, I'm being kissed—
Smack on the jugular. Her fuzzy face,
Her deep fringed wings that spread like lace
Along my shoulder—they make me shudder,
Even if she is my father's mother.

When bedtime comes, it's even worse.
She tells me a story (usually verse)
Then shimmers like a dust cloud's wreck,
And gently settles on my neck,
A constant pain in the you-know-where,
And all night long she suckles there;
She sips my blood and rustles and snores
(Quite loud for a bat) till she rattles the doors.

When morning comes I'm a dismal shade,
Ænemic and pale as a new-laid egg.

So now when she comes I grab my hat
And hide in the empty vintner's vat
Till I hear her departing footfalls' pat—
My Grandma, you see, is a vampire bat.

Lupus-Luna

Something electric, kinetic crackles,
Splits darkness deeper than black shadowed oaks
Can understand, despite their age. Above,
Bone-white wolf-moon waits, weary and wary.

For a heartbeat's breadth, breathing stops as small
Creatures skitter, freeze, anonymity
Their best offense against masked, waiting death.
Bone-white wolf-moon waits, weary and wary.

When it strikes at last, slashing silent pain
Unseen, unfelt almost until red heat
Submerges cooling flesh…still, nothing breathes;
Bone-white wolf-moon waits, weary and wary.

Urgent sounds linger, inexpressibly
Sad, stopped to all but fearful ears. They cease.
For now…for this long night. Dawn promises….
Bone-white wolf-moon waits, weary and wary.

WIROS

Crouching here, dark-shadowed
from heat-searing sun,
this body seems mine … almost —
or I its, I do not know.

I run. The knife piercing my heart
matching the knife heavy in my hand.
Blood streams naked thighs,
flashing crimson as I race —

hot-red from my new kill …
it terrifies … attracts.
Within shadows, my quarry
cowers. It knows I am here, but

not yet who or what.
It fears the phantom-shadow
of bright day, killing and
killing. By night they search

but will not, cannot find,
or know that I hunt with them
as they search, that I
AM the monster — and in sweet darkness,

I will not know it either. Now
I run, naked through the sunset, bleeding

from thorns and briars, heart hammered
by the demon I have become—

hideous body erect,
hairless, clawless, fangless,
slaying brothers. I weep to die,
but cannot.

Day-nightmare, at night blessed
oblivion of reality. With the night,
I will become the wolf
again.

SLEEP...SLEEP....

Sun westering. Clouds knitting against
The coming dark. Sleep. Sleep. Beneath
My hull—grounded as it is on diamond sand—
Small noises as of distant breathing. Waves,
Mere feet from here, settle, die, sleep.
Everything sleeps. Except....
This is the darkness and the curse. Never known
So sharp as at this infinite flick of time between and
Between, daylight dying, night not yet born; and
All around me sleeps...sleeps...sleeps.

When dawn comes, creeping to take me unawares,
I too shall sleep, while all the rest, the life
Around me, stirs, greeting dawn-birds as they sing
Their resurrection from night's grave. All will awaken.
But I—victim of the midnight sleep-thief, sufferer
Beneath the daylight sun....only then will I
Know sleep....

FORSAKEN

white-washed boards streak grey
    where sun and wind have etched
    bleak legacies

wire rusts to grit-rimed dust
    where solemn rain has bleached
    gaunt, lead-dull skies

footsteps fade to riffled grass
    where shadows haunt drab meadows
    you forsook

when fragile ghosts last sang ....

A Short Poem on a *Bubo Virginianis* Escaping with a Torn Wing from a Lycanthrope's Bloody Jaws

Howl owl

TRICK OR TREAT

> "I think that part of being a parent
> is trying to kill your kids..."
> —Arnie Cunningham

This fall, the adults Trick-or-Treat!
Instead of children sheltering innocence
    Behind ghost casks
        Or vampire masks;
Adults Trick-or-Treat. There's no pretence

Of costume here tonight. Beneath
A morbid moon, from door to door they prowl
    Claws cocked for blood,
        Fangs locked to flood
Thirst-ridden throats—beneath blood-moons they howl;

Pale children cower in the dark,
Forget that once, this night, the children fed;
    Forgotten sweets,
        Forgotten treats—
Instead, pulse-pounding heat, rank scent of dread....

Unmasked adults knock , pause...
Claw wooden doors until their children's ears
    Ring with horror,
        Sting with terror—
Children fading as they meet their fears;

Face to face, each adult monster
Mocks its child, bloods its child, devours
    Its child, destroys
        Its wanton toy:
Adult darkness chills the blood-black hours.

BLACKBIRD FALL

Beneath dark storm clouds thundering over
mountain lips, harvest-grains shrivel uncut;
lawns once placid green revert to clover;
and asphalt highways crumble into ruts.
Silence hangs. Promised brightenings hover
unfulfilled. No motion, save fluttered struts
of barren limbs. Dank prodigies cover
sightless windows lurking void and shut.

There should be children, games, kites soaring bright
skies. There should be roiling laughter. Instead,
crows and ravens plump on bitter gall,
rank starlings glitter in their sunset flight,
sable swans glide on lakes as flat as lead,
and bodies lie in state for blackbird fall.

WHERE THE WHITE CROW FLIES

– Dim – dank – scum-clotted ponds breathe
Their pestilence and boil ripe contagion.
Trees – once oak or pine or yew – ease
Raddled branches to a pewter sky, grim

Arms upraised, bone-fingers retching
Ghosts of disembodied needles, leaves,
Insect-clutching galls – punkie, roach-
Infected blots of shadowed life. Stark eaves,

They overhang a dwindled earth – a soil
Barren-blasted – twitching darkness blackness
At its core. And more – … – a distant wail –
Panicked gravity – still warns and wakens

Dead ears. A slice of light – sharded Song –
Surveying its demesne a white crow wings.

HARVEST CROWS

Harvest crows caw dark convocations,
Pace bone-grey walks with skeletal claws,
Haunt suburban entropy and span
Black fingers wide to polluted clay,

Waft contagion through the land. They perch upon
Rough concrete stanchions where lights once glowed at dusk,
Red-eyed, to glare deft retribution. One
Swoops and clicks and snaps diseased flesh that reeks

Beneath an August sun. Another grates
Its challenge for the filament of flesh,
Black flesh, raw flesh shimmering white against
A sable maw. And still the harvest crows press,

And congregate, and lordly strut stilt-gaunt legs
Along flat paths, asbestos drives, dead ways.

CORMORANT

A single cormorant clasps a crippled face
Streaked and freaked with fading ocher stains
Where bird-lime-white once gleamed above a base
Of tumbled rock and patiently sanded grains.

The cormorant unfurls, fed by raging
Need, ragged hunger preying on its flesh—
Unfurls, rises, rides convection waves
Beyond flat swells, until its cliff-face flashes

Once and sinks. For days it rides. Scans the deeps
For shadowed signs, swoops and swirls—and nagging
Blue-harsh static sparks its neurons—ennui creeps—
Its circuit sinks wider lower flagging

Until thick grey voracious ocean currents
Consume the last and final cormorant

SASQUATCH

Come quickly! Look at this,
before the water blurs
its edges.

See....There, beneath
the shadows. It's nearly
gone, but

you can still outline
five toes, a heel—like
but unlike

ours. Some think a hideous
beast has entered our forest,
crouching in

darkness and skittering
out of sight. Some want to
hunt and

kill it, fearful that others
of its kind might hurt
us. But

I say no. What harm could such
creatures ever do—like us
but hairless and only half our size.

*BLOTHISOJAN

Blood-blessing—Germanic
heritage of childlike
blessedness

recalling oak-grove
sacrifices, druid
blood

pouring wine-dark over
stone hollowed pagan
ritual

 [*God bless Mommy,
God bless Daddy,
God bless
God bless....*]

Blessing-blood life-sap
dripping from a world-ash
cross

the light behind a shadow
trapped within
a word

[*Earliest Indo-European form of "blessing"]

HORROR-KU

Town of dead breathing—
dust-centuries twist air;
pyramid-shimmer

Throbbing heat freezes
When the full-moon night arrives—
Vampire's icy kiss....

Baying hounds abrade
Virgin silence with blood-howls;
Vampire stalks again—

Rose-red lips glisten
Without cosmetic blush—a
Vampire's ghoulish smile

Pale white roots wriggle
on moonlight-silvered graves—
The Walking Dead Rise.

Lapis teardrops
Glow in gleaming twilight—
Winged scarabs iridesce.

Souls of Pharaohs speak
Desiccated whisperings—
Winged scarabs whirr

APPENDIX

THE LAST PASTORAL
(KLINGON TRANSLATION)

Translated by Robyn Stewart
Edited by Alan Anderson

[TO THE READER: "The Last Pastoral" contains language and situations that some might find uncomfortable to read.]

From Robyn Stewart to Michael R. Collings:

As I said to the Klingonist who acted as my editor, "I wonder if the ancient craftsmen who produced miniatures for the tombs of kings felt this way: all this work, but no certainty that anyone was ever going to appreciate it." If any one can be trusted to care what happens to a work it would be the author.

The main challenge was the fragmentary quotations. Before this project, no Renaissance poems had been translated into Klingon, and therefore there was nothing to draw on that had even a faintly-remembered-from-grade-nine-English-class kind of familiarity to the Klingon ear. To an English-educated reader, even if a snippet such as "And yonder all before us lie/deserts of vast eternity" is not familiar, it is at the very least recognizable, even to an engineering student, as "some kind of old fashioned poetry." I might have recast your entire poem using recognizable snippets from archaic Klingon works, but then it would have been "The Last Klingon Opera" and not "The Last Pastoral."

I identified the source of each fragment in "The Last Pastoral," because context is essential for Klingon, then translated them, sometimes actually taking overlapping text, because of the needs of Klingon grammar, rhyme or syllable count. (Yes, I managed to preserve AABB rhyming iambic tetrameter).

Your poem uses ellipsis and segue heavily, and also departs from the traditional pastorals in frequently carrying a single thought between lines and even between stanzas. There is probably an actual term for this in poetry analysis, but I think you can understand what I mean. This style was sometimes challenging to translate, because Klingon word order in a sentence is almost invariably Object-Verb-Subject, with most adverbs and locative information preceding the object. Thus a word that comes at the end of an English sentence or phrase may come at the beginning of its Klingon translation. For example, in the fifteenth stanza the phrase "his blood" while referring to the effect of evacuating an occupied airlock, is also a truncation of "his bloody hate abandoned me," completed in the sixteenth stanza. As the subject of a Klingon sentence follows its verb, a truncation of the Klingon equivalent would be /mulon/ ("he/it abandoned me") and nothing to do with blood. It took me a little while to work out what roles "his blood" was playing in that sentence, but when I did I had to come up with something quite different in Klingon. In Klingon culture, to speak to someone of a warrior's cold blood is to reject that person as a mate. So I wrote /'IwDaj bIrqu'mo' mulon/ "he abandoned me because of his very cold blood." The truncation of that, /'IwDaj/, means "his blood", just as the English does.

Thanks to the setting, the vocabulary was rarely a problem. The "scarlet weed" I translated as /naHjej Doq/ (literally "red/orange thistle"). Doq is not a red-orange colour, but a colour that covers the whole range from deep red to orange. "Dirty scuff" I rendered in Klingon as /DI quHvaj/ (lit. "dandruff of debris"), instead of an unwieldy literal translation of "a mark made by dragging or grazing." I was guessing that *scuff* was chosen more for its rhyme with *enough* and its connotation as something unwanted and unimportant than for its exact meaning. quHvaj provided a difficult rhyme, and gave me an opportunity to use one of the more obscure words in our vocabulary. My colleagues call them /Qov mu'/ —"Qov words"—because of my habit of knowing and using them. If Klingons ever used tape-based recording media, the vocabulary is not currently known, so I have translated references to the tape recorder with /Hoqra'/ "tricorder", a Star Trek multi-purpose recording/playback/analysing device. The proper name Newman is transliterated as /nu'man/, which is not known to mean anything in Klingon.

Here is my work, with a literal back translation—don't worry, the Klingon doesn't sound that stilted, I just do it that way to demonstrate the structure—and more explanations. Klingon doesn't have verb tenses the same way as English does, so in most cases if I translate in the past tense, it could also be read as present or future. That is also why you may see more instances of "now" or "at that time" in the translation.

HATLH BOM QAV
The Final Song of the Countryside

[Poem and song are the same word in Klingon. I almost left the title as bang bom Qav—the final love poem—as that would make sense to a Klingon. And "bang bom" is a fun title for a poem about blowing up the Earth. But then I realized, I didn't really know what "The Last Pastoral" meant when I first saw it, so why shouldn't a Klingon have to stop and wonder what the heck a countryside poem is?]

1.
HItlhej, matay', bangwI' yImoj.
'ej nubelmoHlaHbogh Hoch DIpoj
Qu'vatlh! bechjaj marlow, bomDaj je
ghe''or chImqu'Daq bechjaj jay'

Accompany me, we will be together, become my beloved, and we will analyse everything that can please us. %$#%! Let it be that

Marlowe and his poem suffer. Let it be that they &%$# suffer in most desolate hell ...

[ghe"or parallels Hell, being the place occupied by the dishonoured dead.]

2.
naDev jIba'taHvIS, Hoqra'
quvHa' vIQoytaHvIS. QapHa'.
tera'ngan vatlh DIS poH wa'maH
javDIch bommey jatlh.

> *... while I sit here, while I hear the dishonoured tricorder. It malfunctions. It speaks poems of the Terrans' sixteenth century.*

[I broke up long sentences into shorter ones, because Klingon sentences are generally shorter, and also to preserve the segue. Usually the information at the end of one of your sentences was better revealed later than the information at the beginning. You may think it looks as if there more repeated information in Klingon than English, and that is true, too. Klingon pronouns are sometimes vaguer than English, and nouns are short, so it is common to repeat more nouns than you would in English. This doesn't sound redundant in Klingon.]

maqtaH
3.
Hoqra'vetlh. muHlu'pu' 'e' baj
jan ghunwI'qoq. 'a Qo' ... popDaj
Hevba'pu' qoH, luHev je ... QI'yaH
Ghe"orDaq bechjaj Hoch.

> *That tricorder goes on proclaiming it. The so-called programmer deserves to be executed. But no ... the fool has received his/her reward. ... have also received it. &%$#! May they all suffer in hell.*

[The ellipsis in the Klingon precedes the verb.]

peng baH.

4.

SeHlawvam Doq. leQ vIchu'chugh
vaj HughDu'chajDaq jorneb rugh
vIghoD. DaH HughDu' ghajqa'chugh.
ghajbe'.

> *This red control panel fires a torpedo. If I activate the switch*
> *then I would stuff the antimatter of a warhead into their throats.*
> *If they now had throats again. They don't.*

vaj wab vIQoymeH mevbe'bogh

5.

ghoghqoqvetlh maw' vIchu'. yaj'a'?
Heghmo' Newman jIwIvlaHbe'. «tera'
Heghmo' jI'It" jatlh. va! mumobmoH
ghaH. ghu'vam raD

> *Thus I turn on this crazy, unstopping, so-called voice, in order to*
> *hear a sound. Because Newman died I cannot choose. "I'm de-*
> *pressed by the death of Earth" he said. &&%! He causes me to*
> *be alone. He forced this situation.*

'ej lam SIbDoH

6.

buS jay'. Sang'egh 'e' baj lam. jor,
naHjej Doq rurtaHvIS. pIvghor
rIHlaHbogh HoS jaD. Wa"uy'logh
juHDaq nulupmeH yap.

> *and he focused on a %$#@^ satellite of dirt. [I think that's my*
> weakest sentence. I could get a closer translation, but I couldn't

get one that rhymed.] *The dirt deserved to obliterate itself. It exploded, resembling a red thistle. It hurled about energy that could charge up a warp drive. It is sufficient to transport us home one million times.*

bom ghogh

7.
ghuy'cha'! HItlhej, matay'—pagh 'eH
yIHegh, Newman yIDa. ramvetlh
machechbej. ghaHvaD jInepbe'.
vItlhu'moHbe'.

> *A voice sings. Accompany me, we will be together—or die, resemble Newman. That night we were definitely drunk. I didn't lie to him. I didn't tempt him.*

["Sing" was the one fragment I couldn't quite get. "Sing" looked like an imperative, but who or what was being commanded to sing? My editor suggested bom ghogh and I took it because it fixed a syntax error in my Klingon. You can't say just "a million" in Klingon. It has to be "one million" and the extra syllable was driving me nuts. This verse was the subject of a bit of a battle, too. I had a line with partly trochaic meter, and my editor had a fix for it, but it required "yesterday" instead of "that night". Uh-uh. I defended *that night*, as I felt it is very important that the amount of time that has lapsed between events is unknown. Part of my enjoyment of the poem came from speculating on how long it took the narrator to get to this state.]

machechchu' 'e'

8.
vIchID. 'ej pumDI' peng—naS mu',
vISov—machech, maSaghbe'qu'
maH. Hovmey So'bogh DI quHvaj
wIleghqangmeH yapbe' Dotlhmaj.

*I admit we were utterly drink. And when it happened—the word
is cruel, I know it—we were drunk, we were very unsober. Our
state was not sufficient for us to be willing to see the dandruff of
debris that hid the stars.*

[Double entendres are always an issue for a translator, and here a
literal translation of "we were bombed" does not have anything to
do with drunkenness, but a Klingon expression meaning "when it
happened" seemed custom made for this job. The phrase /pumDI'
peng/, literally "when the torpedo fell" served the same purpose as
the bombed pun. I was pleased with this. I also liked the presence of
"that hid the stars" in this stanza. There is a Klingon saying that "If
there are gods they do not help, and victory belongs to the strong,
but all that is seen by the naked stars is remembered" so blotting out
the stars has a spiritual significance, implying preventing the cosmic
memory of an event.]

9.
**chal ngoHlI' pej'eghpu'bogh yuQ,
lunatlhchoHpu'mo' qeHwI' puQ,
Qaw'eghchu' jay'. ghay'cha'. vImaq:
machech.**

*The planet that demolished itself smears the sky because fed up
resentful ones consumed it. It %$#@ utterly destroyed itself.
%$#@! I proclaim it: we were drunk.*

muD Hutlhchu'bogh maSDaq

10.
**cha' tlhuHbogh porghmey qat baS Som.
majatlh maSaQ majach, 'ej nom—
DapollaH pagh DapollaHbe'—
maHotchuq jay',**

A metal hull enfolded two breathing bodies on a moon that utterly lacks an atmosphere. We talked, we cried, and quickly—one way or the other it doesn't matter &^%$# —we touched one another,

[The "metal hull" line doesn't sound awkward in Klingon. It's actually very natural.]

nugh chutHom le'

11.
wIwem. Heghpu'bogh loD maHba'.
nuwovmoH Heghpu'bogh tera'.
vaj maHvaD bIvchoHghach quv 'ugh
HeQnISghachmaj quv tIS.

We violated society's special little rule. We are dead men. Dead Earth illuminates us. Thus for us the breaking is more honourable than our requirement to comply.

[Incidentally, the line "we are dead men" is the first line in the poem that indicates the gender of either person on the space station, in Klingon. I omitted the description of the "pallid" light of earth, because it would have been lengthy in Klingon to establish such a mood for "white"—remember Klingons are vague about colours. The Klingon comparison follows a strict formula, making it syntactically impossible to say that X is more honourable than Y is valid without first establishing a common scale for honour and validity, but I am satisfied that I have adequately translated "more honoured in the breach than valid".]

Qupchugh

12.
qo' naQ, Qupchugh parmaq, Hoqra'
vIQoy. HuH rur, 'oy'vaD qut na'.
'ej pagh wItuQ. yIn porghmaj tuj.

Hegh DaqvaD bIH DItam.

If the entire world were young, if love were young, I hear the tri-corder. It resembles bile, salty crystals for a sore. And we wore nothing. Our warm bodies were alive. We substituted them for the place of death.

vItchugh

13.
Hoch lengbogh wIjwI' jat. vIngagh.
mavempu'DI' mubejchoH. pagh
tuQ. Qam. lang ghaH, 'ej tamtaH ghogh.

If every roving farmer's tongue told the truth. I mated with him. When we had woken, he looked at me. He wore nothing. He stood. He was skinny and his voice remained silent.

["Mated" doesn't have the clinical, barnyard feel as the English. It's more specific than "took", which isn't an idiom in Klingon. "Fucked" or "screwed" would be good translations, but ngagh is neither profane nor slang.]

HIchDalDaq muD wItlhuHpu'bogh

14.
nIjmoH. mubejchu'taH 'ej SaQ.
qabDaj luSIjlaw' Qargh. petaQ!
tera' pIgh rur qab 'e' vIlegh,
SaQmo'. qabvo' boghlaw'lI' Hegh.

He caused air that we had breathed to leak into the airlock. He went on staring at me and he cried. Fissures seemed to slit his face. Bastard! Because he cried I saw that his face resembled the ruins of Earth. Death was being born from his face.

[petaQ doesn't strictly mean bastard. It's an insult but it doesn't discuss parentage, but it's often translated that way.]

15.
**muvaqmeH, wa'logh mon. HIchDal
lojmIt poSmoH 'ej 'oHDaq Sal.
ghIq ngaQmoH, muD lojmoH 'ej tugh
chenHa"egh. 'IwDaj.**

> *He smiled once, to mock me. He opened the door of the airlock
> and went up into it. Then he locked it, caused the air to be gone
> and soon unformed himself. His blood.*

[The Klingon verb chenHa"egh is really hard to translate back into English. We don't have "decompressed" so I went for the image. chen is "take form" -Ha' reverses the meaning "unform" and 'egh turns the subject on itself, but it isn't strictly "unformed himself" as that would be chenHa"eghmoH "caused himself to unform". Bah, it works in Klingon, really.]

'ach jubchugh

16.
**QupwI', SeplaHtaHchugh parmaq
'ej reghlaHtaHchugh 'Iw. SomDaq
naHjej Doq rurchoH, jor. not ngo'-
    chugh belmey,**

> *But if one who was young were immortal, if love could breed,
> and if blood could bleed. He exploded, changing to resemble a
> red thistle on the hull. If pleasures never aged,*

[The *if* has to be repeated in Klingon, making the first fragment very long, so I shortened the second and decreased description in the rest of the stanza. I wasn't extremely happy with splitting a word across lines here, but the interruptions of the pastoral lines are a little chaotic at this point in the poem, so I think I got away with it.]

'IwDaj bIrqu'mo'

17.
mulon! jInoDlaHbej. jIjaq!
vIruch! bortaS vISuq. loghDaq
mubach 'e' nIDchugh vay' jay', tugh
vIghojmoH. not HIDuQ!

> *He abandoned me because of his cold blood. I can certainly re-taliate. I am bold! I will do it! I will obtain revenge. If someone tries to &^%$ shoot me into space, I'll soon teach them. Don't stab me!*

[Some substitutions here, because of the vague idiomatic threats. Regarding "stab": English "fuck" means both "interfere" and "have sex", plus it intensifies the sentence. Klingon curses don't have semantic meaning, let along the same semantic meaning as English ones, but I solved this one with /DuQ/. Literally it means "stab" while figuratively it means "emotionally affect". Then I added /jay'/ which intensifies the way random English profanity does.]

yapchugh

18.
qo'mey wIghajbogh 'ej naDev
mulon 'ej poH 'ej poH not mev.
muHaj. QI'yaH! Heghjaj Hoqra'
bIjaqHa'DI' bIHeSbe'ba'

> *If the worlds we had were enough and he abandoned me here and time and time it never stops. They fear me. %$#@! May that tricorder die. When you were shy you really did not commit a crime.*

19.
bIHeSbe'—yIchu'Ha'!-HeSbe'.
jorneb vIghuSta', bachbeH je

tera' vIpejrupchu', ratlh veQ.
vIQaw'laHbe' ... lojchu'. ram!

> *You did not commit a crime—shut it off! -- not commit a crime. I*
> *have loaded a warhead, it's ready to fire too.*
> *I am ready to completely obliterate Earth, garbage will re-*
> *main. I can't destroy it .. it's completely gone. It's unimportant!*

[The syllables of bIHeSbe'ba' are as follows: bI- indicates first person singular subject, no object, HeS the verb "commit a crime", -be' negation suffix and , -ba' sometimes translated "obviously" a suffix that emphasizes the negation, in a similar way that using "were no" instead of "was not a" does in the English. Note that pejrupchu' can also mean "completely ready to obliterate"]

leQ

20.
yIchu'. SaH 'Iv. chaq rarHa' vogh
pa' poH jub Deb DItu'laHbogh
vaj ratlh peng jay' 'ej jormoH 'ul.
naHjej Doq rurchoHtaHvIS,

> *Activate the switch! Who cares. Perhaps somewhere will mis-*
> *connect the deserts of immortal time which we can observe there*
> *thus the &^%$# torpedo will remain and the current will cause*
> *it to explode, resembling a red thistle,*

["Who cares" in Klingon happens to be homophonous with "Who is there?" I struggled quite a bit with getting the "deserts of immortal time" fragment in there, straying at one point to translating a different line. It had to be a grammatic unit, and fit on one line, and be in iambic tetrameter, and rhyme with something on the first line. My editor came up with vogh - somewhere. "Which we can observe there" is not awkward in Klingon. tu' is the standard verb for stating that something is there, like *il y a* in French or *hay* in Spanish.]

qul

21.
lujaD ... Newman! va! nuqDaq So'?
naDev HIghoS—HImobmoHQo'!
muwuqqa'moHchugh belvam Doj
qatlhej, matay', bang

They will hurl fire about. Newman! %$@! Where do you hide?
Come here—don't make me alone! If these impressive pleasures
change my mind, I will accompany you, we will be together,
bang

[bang is the first syllable of a trucated /banglI' vImoj/ "I will become
your beloved". And of course it's always good to end a poem on a
bang «cue rimshot».]

BTW, there now exists at least one Klingon translation of period
pastoral: I received a framed translation of "A Passionate Shepherd
to His Love" from my editor for Christmas, but I'm still contemplat-
ing whether to retaliate with the obvious "A Nymph's Reply".

If any of this should happen to kindle a spark of interest in the
Klingon language in someone in your classes or your department,
please send them my way. The purpose of the Klingon Language
Institute (http://www.kli.org/) providing translations is to increase
awareness of the language, to attract new people for us to talk to. I
know conquering lands is both a more efficient and more Klingon
way to spread a language, but we work with what we have.

ABOUT THE AUTHOR

MICHAEL R. COLLINGS is an Emeritus Professor of English at Seaver College, Pepperdine University, where he directed the Creative Writing Program for over two decades. He has published multiple volumes of poetry, novels, short fiction, and scholarly studies of such contemporary writers as Stephen King, Orson Scott Card, Dean R. Koontz, and Piers Anthony. His most recent works include *Singer of Lies,* a science-fiction novel; *The Art and Craft of Poetry*; and a Book of Mormon epic, *The Nephiad*, all published by the Borgo Press Imprint of Wildside Press. He is now retired and lives in his native state of Idaho.

www.ingramcontent.com/pod-product-compliance
Lightning Source LLC
Chambersburg PA
CBHW020643180626
46816CB00003B/1104